PRAISE FOR THE QUILT THAT KNEW

Patrick E. Craig has once again written a book that will take you deep into the heart of Amish country. *The Quilt That Knew* is a delightful and intriguing plain and simple mystery.

— VANNETTA CHAPMAN, USA TODAY BESTSELLING AUTHOR

The Quilt that Knew had just the right amount of suspense and mystery. Patrick E. Craig is a great storyteller and keeps you wanting to know more. I cannot wait for the next book!

— SANDY ABD

The Quilt That Knew is another great book by Patrick E. Craig. Jenny Hershberger and Bobby Halverson from the Apple Creek Dreams series are back, but now they are working on a cold murder case. This book had you sitting on the edge of your seat trying to figure out "who done it." Once I started reading it I could not put it down until I finished it. There were so many surprises and twists. First the dead girl in the box, then another dead body found in the woods, and finally the drug overdose of a main suspect. And when Jenny and Bobby start looking at these clues, mysterious things start to happen. This is a "must read" for everyone. I loved this book.

— KAY LEATHERS WINGO

So, how good is *The Quilt That Knew*? Well, I read it straight through in a day! And it's a great start to what will surely be a wonderful mystery series! And my favorite line:

"And I was thinking that the Amish community is not the peachy-keen, perfect world that most people think it is, especially those Englischers who buy those 'Amish fiction' books off the shelf at Walmart. Amish fiction, indeed!"

And, perhaps, my friends, that line best encapsulates what Patrick Craig does best—pure and honest portrayals of the Amish as people with real passions and faults, and not the idealistic fantasies of so many others. And that, is refreshing.

— SCOTT R. REZER — AUTHOR OF THE BUTCHER'S BRIDE, THE LEPER KING AND LOVE ABIDETH STILL

A murder mystery set in an Amish community is surprising in itself; but a story that involves multiple murders? A popular cliche that we hear when discussing old houses is, *if those walls could talk*. In this tale by Patrick E. Craig, the investigators wish the quilt could talk. A retired sheriff and his Amish neighbor are called back to their old stomping grounds to assist in a 40 year old cold case that has been just recently uncovered. Jenny, with her knowledge of the Wooster, Ohio Amish community history finds that her mother's quilting journal is a key component to solving the crime. While trying to narrow the suspects, they encounter another related cold case and have to consider a current murder besides. Stitching all of this information together becomes quite the dilemma and following the action will keep you on pins and needles. Get yourself a copy of this yarn and try to piece it together for yourself.

— CALVIN DOUGLAS SMITH

THE QUILT THAT KNEW

PATRICK E. CRAIG

Cover by Cora Graphics Simona Cora Salardi

www.coragraphics.it

This is a work of fiction. Names, characters, places, and incidents are products of the author's imagination or are used fictitiously. Any resemblance to actual persons, living or dead, is entirely coincidental.

The Quilt That Knew

Copyright © 2022 by Patrick E. Craig

Published by P&J Publishing

P.O. Box 73

Huston, Idaho 83630

Library of Congress Cataloging-in-publications Data

Craig, Patrick E., 1947-

The Quilt That Knew / Patrick E. Craig

ISBN 979-8-9871451-0-4 (pbk.)

ISBN 979-8-9871451-1-1 (eBook)

All rights reserved. No part of this publication may be reproduced, stored in a retrieval system, or transmitted in any form or by any means—electronic, mechanical, digital, photocopy, recording, or any other—except for brief quotations in printed reviews, without the prior permission of the publisher.

Printed in the United States of America

CONTENTS

Acknowledgments   xi
Introduction   xiii

1. Little Girl Lost   1
2. The Call   9
3. The Request   15
4. The Gifts   23
5. Apple Creek Again   33
6. Mama's Box   41
7. Jerusha's List   51
8. Little Girl Found   59
9. Emma   67
10. Go Back To The Beginning   75
11. The Ring   81
12. More Clues   89
13. The Tooth Fairy   97
14. The Truth About Emma   105
15. Maybe... Maybe Not   113
16. Johan Troyer   121
17. Pictures   129
18. A Fall in The Ditch   139
19. Johan's Box   147
20. Jacob   155
21. Case Closed?   165
22. The Littlest Things   173
23. The Quilt That Knew   183
24. Going Home   191

About the Author	199
More Books by Patrick E. Craig	201
The Apple Creek Dreams Series	203
The Paradise Chronicles Series	205
The Islands Series	207

Dedicated to Agatha Christie, the greatest mystery writer ever and the highest selling author of all time... after the Bible of course.

ACKNOWLEDGMENTS

To my lovely wife, Judy, who has walked with me on this writing journey every step of the way and corrected hundreds of pages, spelling errors, and grammatical miscues—and in the process, making me look like I can actually write.

INTRODUCTION

Many of you are very familiar with Jenny Hershberger. You met her in the first book of the Apple Creek Dreams series, *A Quilt For Jenna*. In that story, Jenny was a little girl lost in a terrible snowstorm. Then, in the following two books, *The Road Home*, and *Jenny's Choice*, you came to know her as a grown woman, trusting her God through trials and desperate times. In the first book of The Paradise Chronicles series, *The Amish Heiress*, you met Rachel, Jenny's daughter. In all those books, you also became friends with Sheriff Bobby Halverson, a lifelong family friend, an *Englischer*, lovingly referred to as "Uncle Bobby" by Jenny.

Now Jenny is back in a new series, The Porch Swing Mysteries, and cast in a new role—what I like to call the "Amish Miss Marple." She is living on her family farm in Paradise, Pennsylvania, and Bobby, now retired from being a sheriff, is living with her on the property. She made a name as a historian of the local Amish in both Ohio and Pennsylvania, and became respectably well known by writing some books about the Amish and a column for her local paper titled, "Dear Jenny."

Because she is so informed about the ways of the Amish, she often gets letters asking her for help, especially with unsolved mysteries that have to do with the Amish community. In this first book, Jenny takes on her first case, *The Quilt That Knew*, and with Bobby's guidance and help, she steps into a new season in her life.

Patrick E. Craig

1
LITTLE GIRL LOST

*B*arry Winders watched the bird drop out of the sky and into the woods. His brother chuckled. "You should have steered him to the left, Bee. Now you got to go into Jepson's woods to find him."

Barry scowled. He handed his shotgun to his brother and headed for the edge of the trees. Jepson's woods lay in a rural section between Apple Creek and Dalton, Ohio, and the fields surrounding the woods were prime hunting grounds for pheasant. But the woods themselves near Jepson's pond were still wild and choked with underbrush. To find that pheasant in there would take some work. He looked at his dog and swept his arm across the area in front of him.

"Butch, *hledeg*! Find dead!"

Butch was good. He wouldn't stop until he found the bird. The German Shorthair ran along the edge of the brush excitedly and then caught a scent and bounded into the woods. Barry ran after him. Butch barked, and Barry saw him cutting toward a thick patch of scrub. He followed as quickly as he could. Except for the sound of his feet brushing through the wild grass and the dog running ahead of him, the woods were quiet. It was one of those early fall mornings in Ohio; the trees turning red and gold and enough nip in the air to warrant a down vest. The ground was still damp from the morning dew and the bottoms of his jeans were wet from striding through the tall grass all morning.

Up ahead, Butch was puzzling around the scrub, trying to find a way in. Barry ran up and patted the dog.

"Found him, hey Butch? Good dog!"

The bird was in this patch of brush, and Barry looked for a way into it. He walked around to the right and spotted a small opening. Going down on his hands and knees, he crawled through. Butch followed him, whimpering excitedly. The ground sloped upwards into the center of the patch and it was wet and muddy. As Barry scrambled up the incline, his foot slipped on the muddy ground and slid out from under him. A sharp pain shot through the front of his lower leg. He looked down at his jeans. There was a tear. He pulled his pants leg up. There was a deep gash below his knee that was bleeding pretty good.

"Shoot, Butch, what did I hit?"

Looking down, he noticed a square corner of something that looked like wood protruding from the ground. He brushed away the dirt from around the corner. As he cleared away more dirt and leaves, he saw that he had stumbled over the corner of a box, what looked like a big box, that was buried in the dirt.

"Hey, Billy," he yelled. "I found something. Bring the shovel out of the truck."

In a few minutes, his brother scrambled through into the center of the brush with the old army trenching shovel they carried in the pickup's bed.

Barry pointed. "It looks like somebody buried a big wooden box here. Gimme the shovel."

Barry dug, and in a few minutes, he had uncovered the top of the box. It was big, square, about five feet long, made from wood. Nice wood, like maple or mahogany. The lid was smooth and finished and fastened down into the sides with nails.

"It looks like a chest. Look, the lid has hinges."

"Wow, maybe's it treasure, Bee. Open it up."

Barry pushed the point of the shovel in between the lid and the box and pried up. The lid moved a little. He worked his way down the side and got the lid up all the way on that side. Pushing his fingers into the gap, he pulled. It wouldn't give.

"Billy, pull down there."

Billy grabbed the lid at the bottom and together, the two boys pulled up. The nails in the lid came out slowly with a harsh screech. They pushed the lid over and looked inside. The first thing Barry saw was a flash of color, some kind of blanket. He reached down and pulled on it. Part of it came away in his hand and he jerked back in shock. A very decomposed human face stared up at him.

∽

DETECTIVE ELBERT WAINWRIGHT watched as the team from the Coroner's office pulled the box from the ground, slipped straps under it and walked it back to the ambulance that was sitting in the field outside the woods, lights flashing. Wainwright's sergeant, Gary Pulley, scratched his head. "Find anything, Elbert?"

Elbert shook his head. "No. We spent five hours this morning going over every inch of ground, Sarge. My forensic boys took dirt samples, checked for casings, anything that might be a clue. Nada."

"So, what have you got?"

"Coroner says the body is that of a girl, probably a teenager, about five foot four inches. The back of the skull is badly fractured. Looks like the cause of death was a blow to the back of the head with a heavy, pointed object. The coroner estimates that the body has been in the box for thirty-five or forty years. The box is only five feet long, so whoever put her in had to fold her up to get her in. Because the box was sealed so well, the decomposition was not complete. In fact, it was like she was almost mummified."

"So, there are still skin and hair samples?"

"Correct. They are going to the lab."

"Anything else?"

"A few things. First, the box is made of high-quality hard maple or mahogany. Interestingly enough, and except for the nails in the lid, all the fasteners that hold the box together are wooden pegs. Only a master craftsman, or somebody who builds quality cabinets, does that kind of work."

"Why the nails, then?"

"Somebody was in a hurry to get the body in there and get it buried, so they nailed the lid shut. They probably already had the box. It's a chest or a cabinet of some sort."

"What else, Sergeant?"

"The body was wrapped in a quilt. And it looks like an Amish quilt."

～

ELBERT WAINWRIGHT SAT at his desk and puzzled over the case. He hated cold cases, really hated them. Usually there was absolutely nothing to go on. A body in a box, buried for forty years. An Amish quilt. Nobody was missing around that time, at least nobody reported missing. And what about the quilt? The Amish were notoriously close-mouthed as far as their personal lives were concerned. Why would the murderer wrap the body in an Amish quilt? Where do you start?

The phone on his desk rang. The voice on the other end was familiar. Sheriff Jim Merriweather.

"Hi Delbert."

"Elbert, sir."

"Right, right, Elbert. So, what's going on with the Amish Quilt case?"

Elbert grimaced. Why was the sheriff's department poking its nose in?

"Well, Sheriff, not much so far. Nothing to really go on. A hardwood box, a dead girl who was never reported missing, and a partially rotted quilt."

"So, you checked the missing persons records? No Amish people missing around then?"

"Well, if there were, the Amish certainly didn't say. You know the Amish are pretty secretive about their personal stuff. And if they put someone out of the community by shunning them, they certainly don't let us know. People leave the Amish community a lot and go out into the world. After that they are dead to the Amish and they say little about it. They figure it's their own business. So, a girl who disappeared could just have been thought of as a shunned runaway and we never would have heard a thing." Elbert paused. "Why the interest in the Amish folks, Sheriff?"

"Well, Delbert, I'll put it right on the line. We have an election coming up and if I don't swing the Amish vote, I could go into early retirement, if you get my drift. If the Amish think that I'm ignoring a murder case that has to do with them, they might stay away from the polls more than they usually do. So, I have a suggestion."

"What's that, Sheriff?"

"There was only one man who could consistently swing the Amish vote his way election after election. That was Bobby Halverson. He was a good friend to the Amish and looked after them. In fact, his best friend was an Amish man, Reuben Springer. They were war buddies."

"War buddies? I thought the Amish didn't fight in wars."

"Well, it's a long story. Reuben got tossed from the church just before Pearl Harbor and ended up sharing an apartment with Bobby. When the war came, they enlisted together. It was the dangdest thing. They landed on Guadalcanal together and Springer won the Congressional Medal of Honor fighting alongside Colonel Red Mike Edson. Reuben saved his position from being overrun and killed twenty-five Japanese soldiers single-handedly. He got shot, bayonetted, and clubbed, but he stayed alive and helped keep the Emperor's legions from capturing Henderson Field. Saved the battle, saved the field and saved Guadalcanal, which basically saved the war. When they shipped Springer home, he went back to the Amish church. I guess what happened to him made him realize that war wasn't such a great thing. Anyway, he and Bobby stayed really close. That's what helped Bobby get elected when he ran for sheriff."

"I remember Sheriff Halverson, but what has he got to do with this?"

"Well, I was thinking you might invite Bobby to help you on the case, kind of as a civilian expert. You guys hire them all the time. Bobby could get you in to see a lot of Amish people that would most likely shut the door in your face."

Elbert scowled. He didn't much like people telling him how to run his cases, but when he thought about it, it was actually a pretty good idea. Good for him and good for the sheriff.

"How do I get in touch with Bobby Halverson?"

"He lives out in Pennsylvania on the farm of Reuben Springer's daughter, Jenny Hershberger. And by the way, you might want to get Jenny involved, too. She knows the history of the Amish community in Ohio and Pennsylvania like the back of her hand. She's published books and writes a column that's syndicated in a few national papers. What Bobby doesn't know about Wayne County Amish, Jenny does."

Elbert scowled again. *Boy, this sounds like some kind of Amish Homeward Bound movie.*

"Look, Sheriff, I can go with Bobby Halverson, but getting some old Amish woman involved is a little beyond the pale, isn't it?"

Sheriff Merriweather laughed. "Jenny Hershberger is not some 'old Amish woman, Delbert. She's chain lightning in a dress. One of the sharpest gals I ever met. I've even read her books. No, take my word for it. If you want to get inside the Amish community, you'll put these two on your payroll."

"I think I heard an implied, 'but if you don't' in there somewhere, Sheriff. And it's Elbert."

"Right, Elbert. Well, I'm not making any threats, but your captain and me, well, we've been buddies for a very long time. A word from me could..."

"Yeah, I hear you, Sheriff. I could either end up on the winner's stand, or checking permits at dairy farms, right?"

"Well..."

"Okay, Sheriff, got a phone number?"

2
THE CALL

*J*enny Hershberger gazed out the window of her Pennsylvania farmhouse.
Another fall in Paradise...
Outside the window of her writing room, the leaves had burst into the brilliant red and gold Jenny so loved. It was another part of the cycle that marked the passing of each year, a season that, in the past, had given her great joy and solace. The hot, languid summer months had surrendered to crisp early September mornings. The smell of wood burning in stoves touched the air with ghosts of past falls and winters. She remembered her Jonathan—gone now these several years—chopping wood for the winter months; the sweat beading on his brow and his powerful arms rippling under his shirt as the wood flew off the sharp edge of his axe blade. She thought of her mother and father. This had been one of Jerusha's favorite times, when harvest was over and Reuben was around the house more, helping to put up food for the winter and getting the hayloft filled for the horses. She remembered something her mother had once written, something she had incorporated into her first book—the

book about the wonderful quilt her mother made in memory of her sister, Jenna.

> And then the leaves began to turn gold and red and glow in the setting sun and the fields groaned with the richness of the harvest and the Amish brought their horses and their combines and reaped the fruit of their labors. As at no other time, the reality and necessity of their decision to remain separate from the world came upon the Amish men. Life was work, and work was with their hands and their animals and simple machines that required their constant guidance. They became one with the land, moving upon it in unison, pushing their powerful bodies to the limits of endurance and yet even as they struggled, they rejoiced in the power they had together as masters of their world; a world given to them by a loving God who showed them the way and walked before them—a cloud by day and a pillar of flame by night.

Jenny sighed. She missed her parents—more as the years ran by and the world around her changed with every passing day—she longed for her mother's wisdom and her father's unconditional love. She ran her fingers lightly over the smooth birch wood desk, so lovingly built by her father, Reuben, so many years ago, and scooted her chair forward to begin her overdue column. Jenny looked at the blank paper in the old underwood manual typewriter, waiting for the spark of inspiration to stamp its plain white face with words of wisdom for the masses. She stared at the paper, her fingers motionless. Then, with a sigh, she pushed herself away.

What is wrong with me? I can't write. I don't want to go to the fields; I moon about the house all day...

Jenny Hershberger was an anomaly in the Amish Community —a woman who had married a converted *Englischer*. She was an educated writer who, with the help of another *Englischer*, an author, had published six books. She was also an Amish historian who wrote a column for the local newspaper in which she answered many questions about Amish life and practices. But her present mood made her feel like she was ungrateful for all that God had given her and all the freedom the elders of her community had allowed her, and yet this fall, which should have been a time of great enjoyment for her, had become a season of discontent. She sighed deeply and went to stand at the window.

There was a knock on the front door.

Who can this be?

She went to the door. Through the glass panels that marked the top of the door, she saw a familiar face. She swung the door open.

"Uncle Bobby! You walked down the hill. You usually drive your truck."

Bobby Halverson, ex-sheriff of Wayne County, Ohio, decorated war hero and long-time family friend, stood at the door. He grinned.

"I'm getting old, Jenny. I decided I needed to get more exercise. So, I walked down."

"Where's Rusty?"

"He's sitting in the truck at the top of the driveway, waggin' his tail and waiting for me to drive him down the hill. I guess he's smarter than me."

"Come on in, Bobby. Coffee's on and I need someone to talk to."

Jenny Hershberger was still a lovely woman. At sixty-four, her once flaming red hair was now mostly silvery-gray, with a few remaining red highlights peeking out from under the *Kappe*. There were some crow's feet around her violet eyes and laugh lines at the corners of her mouth, but she had changed little from the girl she had been in Apple Creek, Ohio.

Bobby and Jenny went through to the kitchen and Bobby sat. Jenny brought two steaming mugs of fresh-brewed coffee. Bobby picked up the small pitcher and poured in a generous bit of cream. He took a long pull and then Jenny saw him looking at her.

"What, Bobby?"

"You know, Jenny, there's been a lot of water under the bridge since your mama found you in that car in 1950 in the middle of the big storm. I've watched you grow up, I went with you to find your birth mother, I was there when you married Jonathan and then lost him, and I was there when you found him again."

"That's true, Bobby, but why are you waxing nostalgic?"

"Well, I figure I know you better than anyone knows you, even your own daughter."

"And?"

"What I'm getting at, I guess... is something troubling you?"

Jenny stood up and walked to the window. From here she could see the little house on top of the rise where Bobby had lived since he retired from being the sheriff of Wayne County. Across the drive was the big hayfield where she found Jonathan when he had the stroke that killed him. This was the house that her birth mother, Rachel Borntraeger, had been born in and grew up in. This was the farm her grandfather Borntraeger had given to her and Jonathan when they were married. She had everything she needed... Or did she?

"Why do you ask, Bobby?"

Bobby smiled and set his coffee down. "Like I said, Jenny, I can read you like a book. Over the last couple of weeks, I've been watching. You seem out-of-sorts, distracted, off your feed... It seems like there's no get-up-and-go."

Jenny sighed and went back to sit down. "You're right. I'm feeling out of sorts. Distracted is a good word. I've got deadlines for my articles, but I can't write them—I sit down at the typewriter and stare at the wall. My mind wanders, thinking about the things of the past... Jonathan, my folks. Well, you know."

Bobby nodded. "Yeah, I know how that goes. I miss your dad and mom every day, and Jonathan was like the son I never had."

They sat there in silence for a while. The morning sun poured its beams through the lace curtains. Jenny could see the little dust motes floating in the air.

"I just feel like nothing I'm doing seems to help anyone. I feel... well, useless."

"What about your column? You help people to understand the Amish culture. You give them great recipes..."

"That just doesn't do it anymore, Bobby. How many times can you answer a question like, 'Do the Amish use hot water?' And I can only raid my mother's recipe box so many times before my readers figure out that I've hardly ever cooked a bean. If Jonathan hadn't taught me how to make coffee, I would never be in the kitchen."

"Did you ever think of taking up quilting? After all, your mama was a master."

Jenny laughed out loud. "Bobby, I'm a Borntraeger. I wasn't born a Singer and I'm only a Hershberger by marriage. Borntraegers are farmers, not quilters. The only time my mom ever heard me cuss was when I tried to stitch a straight line on a quilt." Jenny laughed again. "Oh no, quilting is not my cup of tea."

Jenny paused and got serious. "You know, Bobby, I think I need something brand new, entirely different, something I've never tried my hand at."

Just then there was a chiming sound from Bobby's pocket. He reached in and pulled out his cell phone. He looked around. "Is it okay to take this in an Amish house, or do I have to go outside?"

They both laughed. Then Bobby answered. "Bobby Halverson."

Jenny could hear a tinny voice from the other end of the line. She listened as Bobby talked.

"Sure, Detective. I remember you. You were a very wet-behind-the-ears rookie over at the Police Department when I retired."

Bobby looked over at Jenny with a quizzical look on his face.

"Jim Merriweather gave you my number. How's Jim doing? Does he still fit in my chair at the sheriff's office or has his wife's good cooking changed all that?"

Jenny heard what sounded like a chuckle.

"So, why did Jim give you my number?"

Jenny heard another stream of conversation, with Bobby nodding and occasionally adding an "interesting..." or a "Hmmmm..." Finally, he looked up at Jenny.

"Well, Detective, it's an interesting offer... what? Consulting fees? Two hundred dollars a day, plus expenses? Now that makes your offer VERY interesting."

Jenny heard more conversation from the other end.

Bobby nodded, then answered. "So, let me get this straight. You have a murder case that might affect the Amish community, and you want to use me as a go-between to talk to the locals. Is that right?"

Jenny heard the man answer with a yes.

"And since I'm a former sheriff, you can reinstate me for this case as a consultant with police powers?"

Another yes from the other end. Then the man said some more. Bobby looked over at Jenny and grinned.

"Yes, Detective, that sounds like something that might interest Jenny."

There was more conversation from the other end of the line.

"Yes, she's sitting right here. Would you like to speak to her?"

Bobby put his hand over the receiver and grinned. "Be careful what you wish for, Jenny," he said as he handed her the phone.

3
THE REQUEST

Jenny took the phone. "This is Jenny Hershberger."

"Mrs. Hershberger, this is Detective Elbert Wainwright with the Wooster Police Department. I'm investigating a case and I've hit a dead end. I am hoping you and Sheriff Halverson can help me."

Jenny glanced over at Bobby, who had a 'cat-who-swallowed-the-canary' look on his face. "Me? How could I help the police in Ohio?"

"Well, Ma'am, we have a cold case that has become very cold indeed. A young girl was murdered here about forty years ago and buried in the woods out by Jepson's pond in a handmade wooden box. But the crucial clue is the one I was thinking you could help me with."

"What would that be, Detective?"

"The body was wrapped in a quilt."

"And..."

"I believe the quilt is an Amish quilt. It has all the characteristics of one and it is well made. I thought you might help us identify the maker, or tell us who would have been making quilts in the Wooster area back then—being that you're a well known Amish historian and all."

"Well, I'm not sure…"

"To tell you the truth, Mrs. Hershberger, I'm at my wit's end. My captain and Sheriff Merriweather are breaking my back on this one, and I could really use some help. I've asked Sheriff Halverson if he would be the police liaison between us and the Amish community, but I also need someone who is an expert on the history of the Amish around this area. Captain Merriweather says that would be you. I can offer you the same consulting fees as I did Sheriff Halverson, but, of course, with no police authority. Is there any way you could come out and just give me some insight into this?"

Jenny put her hand over the receiver and mouthed to Bobby, "He wants me to come out there and help him."

Bobby grinned and said quietly, "You said you wanted to try something new. Well…"

Jenny sat for a minute, thinking.

"Mrs. Hershberger?"

She took her hand away. "Yes, Detective, I'm here. Let me think about it and talk it over with Bobby."

"Oh, thank you, Mrs. Hershberger…"

"Jenny."

"Thank you, Jenny. This would mean a lot to me."

"We'll talk it over and let you know."

She handed Bobby the phone. He put his hand over the receiver.

"It sounds interesting, Jenny, but I'm retired. I don't know if I want to get back into this, even for one case."

"Oh, no you don't, Bobby Halverson. You're the one who got me into this, so if I go, you go. Besides, it might be fun to see my cousins and visit the old place, and you can go see your sister."

"You know I don't get along with her dead-beat husband."

He took his hand away. "Detective Wainwright? Yeah. It

sounds very interesting. Let me talk it over with Jenny and we'll get back to you soon. What's a number where I can reach you?"

Jenny handed Bobby a pencil and a piece of paper.

"Go ahead. 234-544-2306? That's your office? Home? Sure. 234-543-6626. Okay, Detective, we'll let you know. Goodbye."

Bobby closed his cell phone.

Just then, another knock came on the door. Jenny rose with a quizzical look on her face and went to the door. It was her daughter, Rachel, and her grandson, Levon. Noting the surprised look on Jenny's face, Rachel grinned. "You forgot I was coming!"

Jenny put her hand to her forehead. "Of course, we are going to make *stöllen*. It slipped my mind."

"Mama, you worry me sometimes."

"You're right, Rachel, I am getting forgetful."

"It's not that you are forgetful, Mama, it's just that you think about so many things, that sometimes the little things take less precedence."

Jenny laughed and shook her head. "You are right, Rachel. But being with you is not a little thing. It's just that I've had an interesting request and, of course, my brain went flying off into the land of possibilities. Come in, come in. Your Uncle Bobby is here."

They went into the kitchen. "Bobby, look who's here."

Bobby got up and embraced Rachel with a warm hug. Then he turned to Levon and shook his hand.

"My, my, you're getting old in front of my eyes, Levon."

Levon punched him lightly on the shoulder. "You should talk, Uncle Bobby."

Levon King was almost eighteen now, a tall handsome young man who had joined his father, Daniel, in working the King farm, and now worked Jenny's farm as well. Levon took his *grossmütter* in his arms and kissed her.

"How are you today, *Mütti*?"

Jenny looked at the tall young man and then kissed him back. She smiled at Rachel.

"Your son is a man, *dochter*. And he is so much help to me." She looked at Levon again, appraising the handsome face, the dark hair, the tall, strong, youthful body.

So like Gerald, yet so like Daniel. A St. Clair and also... a King.

"I am surprised you don't have a girl you are courting yet, Levon. The young ladies of Paradise must go all a'twitter when they see you coming."

Levon blushed and shuffled his feet. "*Mütti!*"

Rachel grinned. "He has someone he has set his cap for, Mama."

Levon looked at his mother with surprise on his face. "How do you know that, Mama?"

Rachel shook her head.

"Levon King! I am your mother. Do you not think I see the flush on your face when Amanda Troyer walks by? Do you not know that I see you staring after her like she's one of your papa's fine horses?"

Levon blushed again and looked around. "I... I have to go now, Mama... uh... to get the lumber Papa needs for the new chicken house. I will be back in a few hours."

The young man bolted out of the kitchen, propelled by a burst of laughter from the three adults.

Rachel sank down in a chair. "*Kaffee*, Mama?"

Jenny went to the stove and poured another cup.

"Now, what is this interesting proposal?"

"A detective in Apple Creek has a cold case... is that what you call it, Bobby?"

Bobby nodded. "Well, it's not exactly a cold case because it's only been on the books for a short time. A real cold case is one that has not been solved after a considerable time, but remains on the books. Here, we don't know who the victim is or if they were ever reported as missing. So even though the body has been in the box for forty years, it's really a fresh case."

Rachel looked puzzled. "Body in the box? It sounds pretty horrible."

Jenny nodded. "They found the remains of a young woman in a box buried in Jepson's Woods outside Apple Creek. The detective in charge, Detective Wainwright, has asked us to give him some advice, act as consultants. He's actually putting Bobby back into harness."

"Advice? I understand him asking Uncle Bobby, but why you, Mama?"

"It seems the killer wrapped the body in what appears to be an Amish quilt. The detective seems to think that I can help him determine who made the quilt and perhaps that will lead us to some information about the girl. I'm just not sure I'm quite the right person."

Rachel put her hand on her mother's arm. "I think you will be absolutely the right person to help. After all, you are a historian whose specialty is the Amish of Pennsylvania and Ohio. You found your own birth mother when it seemed there was no way to solve that mystery, and you played a big part in getting me away from Augusta St. Clair when she tried to steal grandfather Robert's money from my inheritance. But you told all about that in my book. When are you going to finish the next ones?"

Jenny laughed. "I haven't had a lot of time for writing lately, but I promise I will get to them. Actually, The Amish Princess is almost finished."

Bobby smiled and took a swig of his coffee. "Don't forget, I was there too, and that's why I'll go if Jenny goes. I think we'd make a great team, and besides, I'm getting bored sitting up on that porch smoking two packs of Camels a day. I need a diversion... and so does your mother."

Rachel scooted her chair closer to Jenny and put her arm around

Jenny's shoulders. "I think you understand a lot about life, and you've learned it by watching the Amish people in our village, Mama. There is a lot that goes on here that the people who read Amish fiction have no idea about. Why, Paradise is like a miniature version of the world. I think all the columns you've written and all the researching you did for your books will be invaluable in this adventure. And... I've been noticing that you've been a little distracted lately—like forgetting I was coming to make *stöllen*." Rachel grinned. "So, I say, go for it!"

Jenny looked at her lovely daughter and smiled. "You're right, Rachel. There are plenty of things that happen here, things that let us know a lot about people and how they think. The *Englischers* think the worst thing that happens to the Amish is when the wheel falls off the buggy of the Cary Grant look-alike *Bisskopf's* son, while he's driving to court the young Amish girl who strangely resembles Grace Kelly. None of which I've ever known to happen."

"You know and I know, Mama, that the Amish have just as many desperate situations in their lives as the *Englischers* do, situations that only *Gott* can handle. I think of my own life..."

A knowing glance passed between the three of them. "So, I say, go help this young detective and see what happens. It may open something brand new in your life."

∽

JENNY SAT in the passenger seat of Bobby's old Ford truck as they cruised down Highway 70 toward Ohio. Rusty was curled up in the space behind the seats, every once in a while letting out a whimper to let them know he needed to get out for a bit. The fall colors of the Midwest had come to life. The buckeye trees had exploded into torches and from time to time, Jenny spotted a 'vee' of geese pointed south.

Many memories filled Jenny's thoughts. She remembered the time she and Jonathan had been running away from some drug dealers who thought Jonathan had their money. That was back in the days before Jonathan found the Lord and came back to his Amish roots. Jonathan Hershberger. Jenny smiled to herself. Bobby glanced over.

"What?"

"I was just thinking about the first day I met Jonathan in Wooster, the day he almost ran me down with that funny old hippy van. And then he got out of the car and he had those striped pants on and long hair and a headband and that leather vest." She shook her head and paused. "He was the most beautiful thing I'd ever seen."

Bobby nodded. "Jonathan had a lot of man hidden under that getup. And it didn't take him long to let it out. A real good guy."

"My papa... oh my. He had a fit when I told him I was in love with Jonathan."

"But he came around, Jenny, like I knew he would. Especially when he saw Jonathan would do anything for you, even give you up if it meant the best for you."

Jenny turned her head to hide the tears that came to her eyes. She looked out the window for a while, watching Pennsylvania roll by. Jonathan had been in her thoughts, especially lately.

I guess they never really leave, Lord. Jonathan, Papa, Mama... they are always with me.

What Jenny didn't know as they rolled along was how much her mama would be back in her life, and soon.

4
THE GIFTS

*D*etective Elbert Wainwright was having second thoughts. He had expected something a little different when he asked Jenny Hershberger to come to Wooster to help him out. So, when the diminutive silver-haired Amish woman with a white *kappe* and a plain blue dress showed up at the station accompanied by a slightly overweight eighty-some-year-old man, he was taken aback.

But Jenny sat down in the chair in front of his desk before he could say anything.

"So, Detective, you say you have an Amish Quilt you want me to look at?"

"Yes, Mrs... yes, Jenny. It's a bit deteriorated... Say, can I ask you something?"

"Yes, Detective?"

"Ma'am, do you think you two are up to handling a police investigation? I mean you're... you're..."

"Old, Detective?"

"Well, Ma'am... I wouldn't exactly put it that way..."

"Stop calling me Ma'am, Detective. I'm Jenny and I'm only sixty-two years old. I'm not even old enough to retire. And Bobby is in great shape for his age. He even started walking down the hill to my house to keep in shape." Jenny ignored Bobby's grin. "So why don't you show us what you have?"

Elbert shrugged and nodded. "Okay, but we have to go to the evidence room."

Together, the trio walked down the hall to the Wooster Police Department evidence room. Elbert nodded to the policeman who was manning the cage.

"I need to look at the quilt from Jepson's woods."

The policeman nodded and went back into the area behind the screened-in section. In a minute, he returned and opened the door to let them into a reviewing room. He handed Elbert a box and left the room.

Elbert opened the box and removed a large plastic bag. Carefully, he opened the bag and pulled out pieces of a quilt, which he gently spread on a long table in the middle of the room. Jenny went to the quilt. There was one large section and several smaller pieces in the box.

"It's like a jigsaw puzzle," Bobby said.

Jenny found the corner pieces and set them in place. Then she looked for the border and arranged them around the edge of the table.

"Detective, Bobby... help me lift the center into place."

The three of them took a corner and lifted the rest of the quilt into the center of the table. Jenny looked at it.

"It's got to be turned over."

Again, they lifted and gently turned the quilt so the top side was now down. Jenny stepped back and looked. It wasn't quite right.

"Grab your corners and turn it clockwise one quarter turn."

They did, and finally the pattern made sense. Slowly, Jenny arranged the corner and edge pieces into a coherent pattern, and as she did, something about the quilt seemed very familiar. "I know this quilt," she whispered.

She walked around the table and lifted the corner pieces and turned them over one by one, looking for something. There it was! A small embroidered heart!

Jenny stared down at the quilt. The beautiful quilt had a deep purple eight-pointed design in the center that spread outward through concentric rings of diamond shaped violet, purple, pale blue, and maroon pieces. The last ring was deep purple and the rays of the star radiated outward from there in a wonderful burst of color. Now it was stained and deteriorating, but then...

The whole star had been laid on a cream-colored backing and the seamstress had embroidered beautiful chambered nautilus shapes in between each arm of the star's rays—almost invisible until you looked closely. Three different borders surrounded the white backing. The inner border was composed of small square boxes with a dark purple border containing maroon, purple, light blue and white flowered strips pieced in rows inside them. Then came a border of white with bouquets of lilacs clustered all throughout. The outer border was purple with green leaves festooning the material and angel's breath flowers filling in between them.

A flood of memories swept over her. Jenny remembered going to the stores around Wooster looking for just the right cloth. Jerusha had given Jenny the job of cutting pieces, but when she asked if she wanted to do some of the stitching, Jenny shook her head. She was not a quilter—her designs were awkward, the edges of the pattern pieces she sewed were puckered.

"Oh, Mama, I will never, ever, be a quilter like you. I just can't do it."

She remembered her mother's comforting arm around her shoulder, and the soft voice that always seemed to soothe her heart.

"Quilting is definitely a gift from God, Jenny, and you do not yet seem to have the eye for it. But you are gifted in so many other ways and your *daed* and I are so proud of you. Don't be disheartened. Sometimes you are a little *eigensinnig und ungeduldig* and, yes, these are qualities that do not fit well with quilting." Jerusha smiled. "You must learn to still your heart and calm the stream of thoughts rushing through your head."

Boy, was that ever me. My mama knew me so well. Still my heart and calm the stream of thoughts—still hard for me, even after all these years. I remember that day—Mama reached down and enfolded me in her arms.

"Sie Sind meine geliebte dochter," she whispered softly into the untamable curls that refused to be controlled by hairpins and happily tumbled out from under the slightly askew kappe on my head.

I turned on my stool, and my arms crept around your waist, Mama. I held on to you as though I would never let go. I listened to the beating of your heart...

"Jenny?"

Jenny came back to the present with a start. "I'm sorry, Detective. I was just thinking... about my mother... What was your question again?"

Elbert smiled. "I haven't asked one yet. But if I had, it would be, what is your connection to this quilt?"

Jenny looked at Bobby and then back at the detective. Suddenly, she had a surprising rush of emotion and tears filled her eyes. She looked away for a moment, then gathered herself.

"This... this is a quilt my mama made. She used to make them for the needy people in our community. We would take them to their homes and leave them anonymously. That was my job. I would carry the quilt quietly up on the porch in a box, ring the doorbell and run." Jenny pointed to the embroidered heart. "Mama would put this little heart on each quilt to remind the people who received one that it was a labor of love. That's how I know it's one of her gifts. Detective, this is a Jerusha Springer quilt!"

∽

BOBBY AND JENNY and Elbert sat in the coffee shop down the street from the police station. Elbert poured some cream in his coffee and then looked at Jenny. "What is the story behind these gifts?"

"My mama... she had what she called her ministry of blessings. She did everything well, but with quilting, she was a master. There wasn't anyone in Wayne County that came close. Once, when she was wondering how she could use the talent God gave her to be a blessing to others, it came to her there might be needy people in town who could use a nice, warm quilt against the winter cold. So, in her spare time, she would make her gifts. She could do a quilt in about a month, but she didn't make one every month. So over the years she made ten, maybe fifteen quilts that she gave away. She would check with the elders of the church to pick the families that were really needy. She tried to remain anonymous, but pretty soon anyone who got a quilt knew who gave it. This is one of those quilts."

"Can you remember who she gave them to?"

Jenny looked back down at the quilt. "I might, Detective. But I'm not sure. It's been fifty years since she made them."

Bobby spoke up. "Can you remember the houses you visited, Jenny? You went with Jerusha and Apple Creek was just a wide spot in the road back then."

"Well, we passed them out over about a five-year period, and I think she did two a year. So that would be ten or twelve families. Let's see... Do you have a pad and paper, Detective?"

Elbert reached into his coat pocket and pulled out a small notepad and a pen. He handed them to Jenny. He went to the window and spoke to the policeman in charge. In a minute, two men brought in some chairs and Jenny sat down. Bobby sat next to her, and Elbert sat across the table. Jenny's brows knit as she tried to remember.

"The Aumans got one, Bernard Kauffman got one for his wife... you remember the Kauffmans, Bobby?"

Bobby nodded. "Very well. Bernard and I used to go pheasant hunting together in the fall."

"And there was Susan Wengerd, Gerard Byler..." She paused. "This is hard. I remember those four families, but there are at least six more."

Bobby unconsciously reached for a Camel in his shirt pocket, then realized he was in the evidence room. "What about Jerusha, Jenny? Would she have made a list somewhere?"

Jenny brightened. "Of course, Bobby. She was so meticulous she would have kept notes. I could have Rachel look in my Mama's quilting chest. In the meantime, we could visit some families that I remember."

"That would be good," said Elbert. "We can go tomorrow. In the meantime, it's getting late, and I want you folks to get some rest."

Jenny stood up. "I'll work on the list some more tonight." She thought about the quilt.

After all these years, Mama...

∼

BOBBY AND JENNY parked the truck and went into the restaurant.

Bobby looked around. "Boy, oh boy. Fisher's Home Pantry. I haven't been here in so long and I'm sure glad it's still here. Best cherry pie in the world."

"Bobby? Bobby Halverson?"

They turned. A plump, elderly Amish woman with a black kappe and dress was staring at them.

"Hello, Geraldine."

"Bobby Halverson! *wunderbaar!* So many years." She looked over at Jenny. "And Jenny Springer! I mean... I mean Hershberger, of course. My land, it is so good to see you both." She stepped over to Jenny with her arms outstretched. Jenny slipped into them easily.

"Hello, Mrs. Fisher. It is so good to see you."

"What are you two doing in Apple Creek? I thought you were out in Pennsylvania with the real Amish." She smiled, and they all laughed.

Bobby put his arm around Geraldine's shoulder. "If you bring over two of your biggest pieces of cherry pie with lots of coffee and fresh cream, we'll tell you all about it."

"You got it, Sheriff." She pointed. "Go sit over there in the corner booth." Geraldine bustled off while they found their way to the booth. In a minute, she was back with two enormous pieces of warm pie and two cups of steaming coffee. Bobby noticed the scoop of ice cream melting in the middle of each piece. He grinned. "You didn't forget."

Geraldine blushed. "You always loved ice cream on your cherry pie, Bobby."

"It's one thing I have really missed. And how's Fred?"

Geraldine smiled a sad smile. "Fred's been gone for two years. He had a heart attack."

Bobby motioned for her to sit. She slid in beside Jenny.

Jenny leaned over and put her arm around Geraldine. "I'm sorry, Mrs. Fisher. I always loved Fred."

"And he loved you. There was no one else who knew the history of the Amish like you did. He loved the times when you would share what you were learning."

Geraldine's daughter appeared and handed them a large pitcher of frothing cream. Bobby poured some into his coffee.

"So, what brings you back to your old home?"

Jenny glanced at Bobby, who nodded. "We are helping a local police detective with the Jepson's woods murder case."

"Ah, the girl in the box. It's all over the Amish community. We were worried that the police would do nothing about it. But how are you involved in the case?"

"Well, it's really because of the history that I'm here. Detective Wainwright…"

"And Sheriff Merriweather…" interjected Bobby.

Jenny smiled. "… And Sheriff Merriweather… thought that we could be of help. Me, because the quilt that was wrapped around the girl was an Amish quilt and he thought I might know who would have made it. I was surprised to discover my mother made the quilt."

Geraldine shook her head. "Land sake's, your mother, you say."

"Yes, it was one of her ministry gifts she gave to needy people."

"Isn't that something? One of your mama's quilts. You know, everyone in Apple Creek loved your mama. And we all knew about her 'gifts' even though she tried to keep it a secret. So unassuming, and such a wonderful quilter." She paused, then looked at Bobby, who was polishing off his pie.

"And you, Bobby?"

Bobby wiped his chin with a napkin. "Well, Jim asked me to come along to be a liaison to the Amish community."

Geraldine nodded. "That's right, there's an election coming." They all grinned.

"Nobody knew us like you, Bobby. That's why we always turned out in November. Sheriff Merriweather would do well to get to know us like you did. But then he doesn't have a friend like Reuben."

There was a moment where each of the people at the table remembered Jenny's papa, each in their own way.

Bobby broke the stillness. "Do you think I could get another piece?"

"Coming right up."

THE GIFTS

∼

The phone in Jenny's room rang. She awoke from a troubled dream where she was chasing girls wrapped in quilts through Jepson's woods… running, running, but she could never catch them… the phone rang again. Jenny rolled over and looked at the clock. It was 4 a.m. She shook herself awake and reached for the phone. When she picked it up, there was silence on the other end.

"Hello?"

Jenny could hear breathing, a soft steady sound. "Hello?" she said again.

"You need to go home." The voice was muffled, harsh.

"What?"

"You need to go home and forget about the girl."

"Who is this?"

"Let her rest. She's been dead for forty years. She was no good. It's better she's dead."

"Wait a minute, who is this?"

"Just go home… before it's too late."

There was another pause and then the voice.

"Es könnte sehr gefährlich für Sie sein."

The line went dead.

5

APPLE CREEK AGAIN

*J*enny sat in the motel restaurant with Bobby. It was early, 7:00 a.m. She stared down at the coffee cup between her hands.

"The person spoke German, Bobby. Who speaks German but Amish people?"

"They told you it could be very dangerous for you?"

"That's what they said. The voice... well, it was muffled and distorted... harsh, like they were disguising it. Maybe with a towel or a cloth. I couldn't really tell if it was a man or a woman." She looked up. "What have we gotten into, Bobby?"

Bobby put his hand on Jenny's. "Don't worry, Jenny. I'll let the detective know and have him put a stakeout on the motel. I will also have us moved to adjoining rooms with a door between. I'll be very close, and so will this." He patted his coat under his arm, and for the first time, Jenny noticed the slight bulge.

Bobby saw the look in her eyes. "In answer to your unspoken question, yes, I am totally licensed to carry a concealed weapon. And... I still know how to use this. And... I think the perp made a mistake."

"What do you mean?"

"If they hadn't of called, we would never know what we know now."

"And what is that?"

"Well, what we know is that the murderer is still around. Or someone who knows who did it and doesn't want the truth to come out. And we don't really know if the person was Amish."

"But they spoke German."

"In the police world, that's what is known as a 'red herring.' The problem with crooks is that they always think they are smarter than everyone, including the police. Their arrogance most always leads them to make a mistake. Another thing they don't think about is that the police are highly trained professionals. They may seem slow and plodding, but I can guarantee you that most of the cops I know, once they get on a trail, they follow it like a bloodhound. So, our mystery perp may think they've covered up the crime, but in attempting to scare you off, they just uncovered themselves. So, they might be speaking German to put us off the scent. You can't live in Apple Creek without picking up some German."

Jenny nodded. "That's true. But how did they know where I was?"

"That's the easiest part. This is Apple Creek, remember? Nothing goes on here without everybody finding out, eventually. They could have called the motel earlier and asked if you were staying there. And there are few motels right in the village, so it would not have taken him long to find us."

Jenny looked up as the girl came with their breakfast.

"But that said, do you want to go home, Jenny? I'm sure the detective would understand."

Jenny was quiet for a minute, then shook her head. "No. I can't go home. I think, somehow, the Lord is in this. Whoever they are, they have to pay, so we need to find out who did this. That young girl has been lying in that box all these years with her killer going scot free. And because it's my mama's quilt, there's a personal connection for me. I think we are here because we are the only ones who can find the answers. And I also think that the Lord doesn't like loose ends in people's lives. Somewhere out there is a mother or a brother or some family member that has wondered all these years what happened to her. And we can help them."

Bobby nodded.

"So, no, Bobby, I don't want to go home." She looked down at the stack of buttermilk pancakes on her plate. Despite her unease, they looked very good. She looked up. Bobby had already started on his.

~

BOBBY AND JENNY drove up the long driveway to the Auman farm. Elbert followed in an unmarked car. An old man with a long white beard came out on the porch. He shaded his eyes against the fall sun and tried to see who was in the old truck. Bobby pulled up at the front porch and he and Jenny climbed out.

Bobby raised his hand in greeting. "Howdy, Milt, how's it going?"

"Sheriff Halverson? Is that you? Well, by golly, how are you? What's it been, ten, fifteen years?"

"Well, I've been retired at least that long and I've been in Pennsylvania for ten years, so, yeah, it's been a while."

"Who's that with you?" The old man stepped off the porch and approached them.

"It's Jenny Hershberger, Mr. Auman... My maiden name was Jenny Springer."

"Jenny Springer, well my goodness, this is a surprise." He turned to the door. "Mama, *Kummen sie herein!* We have guests, old friends! Sheriff Bobby and Jenny Springer."

Just then, Elbert walked up. Bobby motioned him up on the

porch. "This is Detective Wainwright, Milt. We are helping him with a case."

"A case?"

An elderly woman came to the door and, seeing Jenny, opened the screen and came out. "Jenny Springer, my lands. *wunderbaar!* It's so good to see you. I have not seen you in so long. *Kumme, kumme.* I have strudel on the table, *Mit kaffee.*"

Elbert hesitated. Bobby grinned. "It's okay, Detective. The Amish won't eat you."

Elbert shook his head. "I have to go downtown to see about another case. I just wanted to meet these folks."

Milt nodded. "Well, if you're a friend of Bobby Halverson, you are welcome here any time."

"Thank you, Mr. Auman." Elbert turned and walked back to his car.

The rest of them went inside and followed Mrs. Auman into the kitchen. The delicious smells of fresh baked bread and strudel filled the room. Bobby looked at Jenny.

"Now I know why I came back."

"*Setzen sie, setzen sie.*"

They all pulled up chairs while Mrs. Auman bustled about, dishing up strudel in bowls with cream on top and bringing cups, which she filled with steaming hot coffee.

Milt took a sip and then looked over at Bobby and Jenny. "*Zo, was bringt sie hier* to Apple Creek? I thought you *ver* planted in Pennsylvania."

Jenny, in the middle of taking a bite, looked over at Bobby. He put his coffee down. "We are helping the detective with an unsolved crime. It involves a quilt that Jenny's mother made many years ago, one of the quilts that Jerusha made as gifts for people in the village."

Mrs. Auman looked puzzled. "A quilt? How does that match with a crime?"

Bobby took a long sip. Jenny took over. "You see, Mrs. Auman, a young girl was found in the woods buried in a box."

"*Ach du lieva.* Yes, we heard. That is terrible. But where does the quilt fit in?"

"They wrapped the girl in it. A local policeman asked me to look at the quilt and I discovered it was a quilt my mama made, one of her gift quilts."

Mrs. Auman nodded. "*Ja,* your mama gave me a quilt many years ago. Milton had broken his leg and was laid up. We were having a hard time keeping the house warm in the winter because we had no money. When your mama gave me that quilt, it kept Milton much warmer and helped him get well."

"Do you still have the quilt, Mrs. Auman?"

"*Naturlich!* Would I give such a gift away?" She got up and left the room. In a few minutes, she returned holding a bundled-up quilt. She laid it on the table. Jenny recognized it right away. She stood up and went to the table. The quilt was beautiful, with circles in crème-backed patterned boxes. Each box was bordered with a wide blue band. Where the bands intersected there was a red square sewn on. A lovely pink border surrounded the whole quilt. As she touched the quilt, a memory of her mama came into her mind.

> *It's called a Vintage pattern, Jenny. We are going to make 42 squares surrounded by a pink border. Inside each square will be a circle made up of eight pie-shaped pieces. You will make the template for the circles for me.*
>
> *But how, Mama?*
>
> *See the bowl I brought from the kitchen? It is exactly ten inches in circumference. Once you have the forty-two squares cut out, you will turn them over, place the bowl on the back and trace around it for a perfect circle...*

Jenny looked up at the people standing around the table. "It's called a Vintage pattern, Mrs. Auman." Jenny smiled. "I cut all the circles for my mama and then cut them into pie shapes. There are forty-two of them, but I confess I had to do forty-nine circles because the first seven were crooked. But I finally figured it out. I was not the quilter my mama was."

Mrs. Auman patted Jenny on the arm. "You may not have been a quilter like her, but you have your own endearing qualities, my dear. We have always loved you, since you were a little girl."

"Even when I scared your cat and she wouldn't come out of the barn loft for two days."

Mr. Auman chuckled. "*Ja, ja*, dat ol' cat. You couldn't help dat *du vas zo enthusiastisch.*"

Mrs. Auman smiled. "She got over it."

Jenny looked at Bobby, who was trying hard to suppress a grin. "My mama used to try to help me calm myself, but my mind was always going a mile a minute. Still does."

They all laughed.

Then Mr. Auman got serious. "Do they know if it was an Amish girl?"

Bobby answered. "There's no way to determine, Milt. There were no clothes, just the quilt wrapped around her. And there were no Amish girls reported missing, at least that we know of."

Jenny paused and then went on. "Do you remember if there were any shunning around then where a girl may have left home and it was never reported?"

The old woman looked at her husband and then shook her head slowly. "No, we have had some shunning over the years, but they were mostly temporary. Once the offender saw the error of their ways, most of them repented and came back to the church. Mostly it was young girls and boys who got a little confused during *Rumspringa* and decided they liked the world pretty good. But for most of our young people, drinking and running around soon wore thin. I only know of one girl who left the church to marry an *Englischer*. She lives in Wooster and I know her mama goes over to visit her to see her *Enkelkinder*."

Mr. Auman nodded. "*Ja*, she does not think we know... but we do, and most of us turn a blind eye. The Amish are not so stiff as the world thinks we are."

Mrs. Auman stood up. "*Und jetzt, Kaffee?*"

~

BOBBY AND JENNY pulled up at the motel. It had been a day of mixed emotions. They had visited four Amish families, each of which still had Jerusha's gift quilt and considered it a family treasure. Memories of her mother flooded Jenny as she looked at the different quilts. Each one was a shining example of Jerusha Springer's work—the finest quilts ever made in Ohio. Besides the Auman quilt, there was a Two by Two Stripe Quilt Jerusha made for Bernard Kauffman, a Jacob's Ladder Quilt she stitched for Susan Wengerd, and a Wander Woods Quilt she had given to Marsha Troyer's little girl, Wanda.

As they sat in the car in the parking lot of the motel, Jenny felt very teary. She wiped her eyes with her handkerchief.

"My mother learned to quilt from her *grossmütter* Hannah. She was good at it from the very first day she sat down to learn."

Bobby nodded. "I remember the first time Reuben introduced me to Jerusha. He was so proud of her, but he was always careful not to encourage her to be proud about her skill."

"Mama was very conscious of how easy it would be for her to slip into pride. That is why she made the gift quilts and gave them anonymously. But they were so good—no one made quilts like my mama. And everyone knew where they came from. She often told me how Great-grandmother Hannah would coach her as she learned..."

If the quilt is going to be even and symmetrical, the cut pieces must be true...

"She let Mama try her hand, and even on her first try, my mother cut the pieces straight and perfect. Mama always listened and learned. When I tried to quilt, she would remind me if the quilt was not aligned properly. Even in just one small part, the whole thing would look off-balance and might pucker. If the design was to be even and pleasing to the eye, each individual piece of fabric must be stitched together just right in order for it to fit together properly. Mama told me to trust my eye and sewing skills for measurement and accuracy. It is a gift not every quilter has. I learned that the hard way..."

Bobby smiled. "I remember when Jerusha showed me her first quilt. She was so shy about showing me, so I tried to not go overboard. But it was mind-blowing. I had never seen any sewing so beautiful. I remember your papa standing by, trying to look stern, but I could see in his eyes how much he loved Jerusha..." Bobby reached in his pocket and pulled out a hanky to wipe his eyes. "Now I'm getting emotional. Let's go eat."

6
MAMA'S BOX

"Yes, Mama, I know where *grossmütter's* quilting box is. Sure, I'll get it out."

There was a pause. "Ship it to you? No, I don't think I should ship it. Something could happen to it and it's too precious. I think I should come there and bring it." Rachel listened. "No, I won't come alone. Daniel will bring me."

Rachel glanced out of the phone shanty at Daniel, who was nodding his head.

"Why should I be careful, Mama?" Rachel glanced at Daniel again.

"You got a threatening phone call? Mama, what's going on over there? Are you going to be all right?" Rachel turned and motioned Daniel to come in. She put her hand over the receiver.

"Mama got a threatening phone call about this case she's working on. I want you to talk to her." Rachel handed the phone to Daniel.

"Jenny, this is Daniel. What's going on out there?"

Rachel heard her mother's voice as she conversed with Daniel. She raised her shoulders and mouthed a "What?" at Daniel. Daniel shook his head and put his finger to his lips.

"Okay, Jenny. I know Bobby's there. Do you need me to come and stay, too?"

More conversation from Jenny's end.

Daniel nodded. "*Ja*, we'll bring Jerusha's box and then, when we get there, we'll see what's happening." A pause. "Well, I'll decide that after I talk to Bobby." Another pause.

"Okay, Jenny, we're coming by train. We should be there by Wednesday. Okay. Yes, we'll be careful. What? The two folders on your desk? Sure, I'll have her bring them. Okay, see you then."

Daniel hung up the phone and turned to Rachel. "I think your mama has gotten into something that's a little more than she expected. She got a threatening call telling her to give up the investigation and go home."

"What does that mean, Daniel?"

"What it means, honey, is that whoever killed that girl is still around Apple Creek and they don't want to be found out. But like Bobby told Jenny, they should have kept their mouth shut."

"Why?"

"Because now they know the killer or someone of interest in the case is still out there. If they had said nothing, the police might have given up."

Rachel thought about that. "Maybe…"

"Maybe what, Rachel?"

"Maybe the killer is someone who knows my mama, or at least knows about her—someone who knows she won't give up on anything she starts. Maybe that's why they came out of hiding. Maybe it's someone my mama actually knows from when she lived there."

Daniel's eyes opened wider. "That's a good point, Rachel. We've got to get to Apple Creek. Jenny could be dealing with a wolf in sheep's clothing." They started for the buggy. "Oh, by the way, Jenny wants you to bring the folders with her Amish newspaper articles in them."

MAMA'S BOX

~

Bobby and Jenny stood on the platform of the Depot Street train station in Apple Creek. Jenny looked around and then a memory came into her head.

My mama was standing in almost this exact spot when I came home after I thought Jonathan died in the boating accident. And now my daughter is coming here and I'm standing in almost the same spot...

She shook her head. Bobby caught the movement.

"What, Jenny?"

"My mama stood right here waiting for me to come home after Jonathan disappeared. And you..." she pointed to the parking lot by the station... "you pulled up in your sheriff's car right over there, where your truck is parked. It's déjà vu."

Bobby smiled. "Man, a lot of water under the bridge since then, Jenny. A lot of water..."

Far down the tracks, Jenny heard a train whistle blow. Around them, a press of people waited for the train. Jenny took hold of Bobby's arm as the train slowed for its final approach into the village.

Diesel engines hummed, wheels clattered over tracks and then the train pulled slowly into the station. Two conductors swung down off the platforms between cars and assisted people off. Jenny scanned the faces of the people clambering down off the train. There! There they were—Rachel, her lovely face, her auburn curls peeking from under her white *kappe*. Beneath her arm was a large case bound with leather straps.

Jenny waved and then waved again. Rachel looked up and a big smile crossed her face. She turned to the blonde giant standing above her on the steps and he smiled and waved. They were walking across the platform, making their way through the crowd.

Then three things happened at once. Jenny stepped forward to take Rachel in her arms, Rachel bent down and placed the box on the platform and a young man who was standing behind them grabbed the box and took off running across the platform.

"Hey! That's my box! Daniel! Stop him!"

Without hesitating, Daniel leaped after the kid. Bobby was right behind. Daniel chased him across the platform, jumped down, hurdled some bushes, and followed him into the parking lot. The thief tried to dodge behind cars, but Daniel was right on his tail. He was almost up to the young man when the thief turned and threw the box at Daniel's feet. Daniel paused for a moment to pick it up and when he looked, the young thief was disappearing into an alley. Daniel ran to the alley and looked all around, but the thief had disappeared.

Jenny saw Daniel coming back with the box and breathed a sigh of relief. Daniel and Bobby climbed the stairs up to the platform. Bobby was red in the face and puffing.

"I'm sure glad Daniel was here. I am too old for foot races."

Jenny took the box. "Thank you, Daniel. I am grateful you were here, too."

Daniel nodded and put his arm around Jenny. "What was that about?"

Jenny shook her head. "I don't know." She looked at Bobby. "Do you think he knew what was in the box, Bobby, or did he just steal it?"

Bobby scratched his head. "That's hard to say, Jenny. He may have just been an opportunistic thief, waiting in the crowd to see what he could pick up."

"But if he was after my mama's gift list, how did he know?"

Bobby looked at the box. "Well, you mentioned your mama made a list of her gift quilts when we were visiting the Amish families yesterday, and that Rachel was bringing it to Apple Creek. And you know how fast information can circulate among the Amish. So, if the person knew about the list, they must have heard it through the Amish grapevine."

Rachel took her mother's arm. "See, it's what I said to Daniel.

Maybe the killer is someone who knows you, who knows that you are a bulldog when it comes to solving a problem or answering a question. So, they must be Amish, or at least close to the Amish community."

Jenny looked thoughtful. "That's a little scary, Rachel, because you could be right. Here we've come back after all these years to investigate a murder that the killer thought would never come to light. And they've been living here hidden away, thinking they got away with something terrible."

"Rachel may be right, Jenny," Bobby said. "So that tells us a couple of things."

"What, Bobby?"

"From now on, we have to play our cards close to our chest. Obviously, the killer has an inside track around Apple Creek. Anything we say, be it during our investigation, or even while we are out at a restaurant, is liable to be heard and circulated. From what I gather, the Amish here are very concerned about this case because it reflects on their community. So, they are all going to be talking about it."

"Which means," Daniel interjected, "that anyone near to the Amish could pick up any information we let slip."

Rachel turned to Daniel. "We?"

Daniel grinned. "You don't think I'm going to let your mother stay here without someone that can run a little faster to help her?"

Bobby chuckled. "Okay, okay, don't rub it in. There was a time, though..."

Jenny nodded. "I think you are right, Daniel. It would be good to have you here."

Daniel put his hand on Bobby's shoulder. "Like old times, eh, Bobby?"

Bobby nodded. "Yeah, that was an adventure, wasn't it?"

Rachel slipped under Daniel's arm. "If you two hadn't come to save me, back then, and Papa, too, there would be no Daniel and Rachel, no Levon, no Sarah and no Lincoln."

Jenny smiled. "I thank the Lord every day for both of you, and for the help you gave us to bring our Rachel home."

Bobby smiled. "So here we are again. We probably need to figure out a place for Daniel to stay... and we need a headquarters where we can talk things over without being overheard."

"Daniel? Don't you mean Daniel and Rachel?"

"But honey, it might get a little dicey around here."

"I'm a big girl now, Mama. What part of my life I can't take care of, Daniel can."

Bobby grinned. "Okay, so we need to talk over some logistics and the best way to do that is over a bowl of hot Amish beef stew. Grab your luggage, kids. The truck's over there. Let's go eat."

～

THE NEXT MORNING, they all met at the restaurant in the motel for breakfast. Daniel was rubbing his neck. "That's not a comfortable mattress, I can testify."

Jenny smiled. "I think I have the question of our headquarters solved. My cousin Jarod Hershberger came by the motel this morning. I sold your *grossdaddi's* house to his father when I moved back to paradise with Jonathan. Jarod's papa died and Jarod inherited all the property, including the old Hershberger farm next door where Mama grew up. Right now, my papa's house is standing empty, so he offered it to us as a place to stay while we are in Apple Creek. Imagine. I'll be back home."

Rachel smiled. "*Wunderbaar*. I remember that house. And I remember the wonderful times I had with *Grössdaddi* and *Grossmütter*. When can we go?"Wunderbaar

"Well, Jarod said he is just finishing up some repairs today, but we are welcome to come tomorrow morning. He will have everything ready for us."

∼

THE SUN WAS high in the sky when the truck turned into the drive leading to the old Springer house. Jenny looked around her. Everything was exactly the same as the last time she had visited—the little white house looked clean and neat, her mama's rose gardens and hydrangeas still edged the green lawn, the front porch held the white swing where she sat with Jonathan many years before, wondering if they would ever be together... nothing had changed, and that felt safe to Jenny.

Her cousin, Jarod, pulled his buggy up behind the truck. He climbed out and Jenny went to him.

"It's so beautiful, Jarod. Nothing has changed. It looks just like it did when Mama was alive."

Jarod blushed and shuffled his feet. "Your mama was a wonderful woman. We all loved her. She and Reuben kept this house so beautifully that we saw no reason to change anything. My dad and mom lived here until they passed, and my mom dedicated herself to keeping Jerusha's memory alive by tending what was already here. Even the furniture is the same."

Jenny took Jarod into her arms and whispered in his ear. "I will never forget how well your family has kept this house. You don't know how much it means to me."

"*Ja,* you are welcome as long as you want to stay. Papa and Mama are gone, and Emily and I have moved to the big house. We have another *kind* on the way and we need more room. This will be seven for us."

Jenny walked across the lawn to the front porch. Off to the right of the porch was the path that led to the bridge across the small creek that flowed between the Springer farm and the Lowenstein's place. As she looked, she saw a familiar figure crossing the bridge. The tall man waved to her.

"Hello, Jenny! Welcome home!"

The words pierced Jenny's heart like quick pinpricks, but she smiled bravely and waved back as the man came across the lawn.

"Henry? Henry Lowenstein?"

"Yep, still alive and taking nourishment." Henry paused. "I just came by to see you and to tell you how wonderful it is to see you back here." He pulled his old baseball cap off and stood awkwardly, holding it in his hands.

Jenny touched Henry on his arm. "Thank you, Henry. That means a lot to me. You've been my friend ever since I was a little girl, and this makes my homecoming perfect."

Jenny gave Henry a quick hug and a kiss on the cheek. Henry blushed and looked down at his feet. Rachel came up on the porch.

"Do you remember Henry, Rachel?"

"Oh, I sure do."

Rachel pointed at the porch ceiling.

They all laughed.

Henry grinned. "I'm a little old to be lifting you up anymore, Miss Rachel, but I sure remember. And you too, Jenny."

"I remember, Henry," Jenny said with a smile as she walked up on the porch.

"And your little sister, Jenna, loved it when I put her up to the ceiling. 'Up, Henny,' she would say. That little girl would have kept me out here all day, putting her up and down, if I would have let her."

Jenny felt a sudden rush of emotion as she remembered Henry with her daughter. Some things never change... But some do.

She walked down the porch to the old swing. It was still there. She sank down into the cushions.

Jonathan and I used to sit in this swing for hours and talk about the future. And whenever I had a problem or something to work through, I would come to the porch swing. Hello, old friend...

She got up and walked into the house.

Through the front door, past the fireplace, down the hall, and into my room... so strange to be back again...

Jenny stood in the doorway of her room and looked in. This room had been her refuge all her childhood, the only place on earth where she felt totally safe. Every night when she was growing up, she knew that her big, strong papa was right in the next room, and her mama was only a call away. That knowledge had kept her secure through all her years.

Jenny put down her luggage and knelt by the oiled oak chest that her papa had made. He had rubbed it with mineral oil, and the smell was woven into the fabric of her childhood.

She put her head down on the wood and closed her eyes, as she felt two tears course down her face. If only the familiar smell of the chest could somehow take her back in time to the small world of childhood—those wonderful days of innocence when life was Apple Creek and the barn and the land and this house, when her mama and papa and Jesus were the center of all things in this house and life passed not in days and hours but in smells and discoveries and colors and seasons, and all her life was surrounded by joy and peace and love.

Bobby peeked in. "You okay, Jenny?"

"Yes, Bobby, I'm very okay. It's just so good to be home..."

7
JERUSHA'S LIST

Jenny awakened early the next morning and lay still in the bed for a long while. The rising sun, peeking over the eastern hills, sent beckoning rays in through the lace curtains that filtered the light. At last, Jenny sighed and then rising quietly from her bed, she threw a shawl around her shoulders, left her room, and tiptoed down the hall. Rachel and Daniel were still asleep in her parent's old room and Bobby was in the guest room.

She opened the front door and stepped out onto the porch. There was an autumn chill in the air, and she pulled the shawl tighter around her shoulders. The leaves on the trees surrounding the house were vibrant with gold and red in the filtered dawn-light and the grass of the lawn had that slight gilded tinge that meant the yard was going to sleep until the spring warmth awakened it. She looked out across the land her family had farmed for over one hundred and fifty years, and a great longing arose in her heart.

"Papa," she whispered.

The fields beyond the road groaned with the richness of the harvest, and she could remember the Amish men, her *daed* among them, bringing their horses and their combines to reap the fruit of their labors. As at no other time, the reality and necessity of their decision to remain separate from the world came upon the Amish. Life was work, and work was with their hands and animals and simple machines. They became one with the land, moving on it in unison, pushing their powerful bodies to the limits of endurance. Yet even as they struggled, they rejoiced in the power they had together in a world given to them by a loving God.

Reuben worked dawn to dusk beside the other men as they moved from field to field, harvesting corn, wheat, potatoes, and barley in abundance. Often the men stopped at the end of a day and stood with their hats in their hands while the sun set in the west, and they sang together of God's goodness and blessing. Jenny remembered her father coming home at the end of the day, his face stoic, but his blue eyes alight with love for his wife and his daughter.

The screen door creaked behind her and she turned. Bobby was coming out with two cups of coffee in his hands. The heat from the cups met the chilled air and an aromatic steam rose, a steam that assailed Jenny's senses with more memories.

Bobby smiled. "Thought you might need a wake-up."

"Oh, yes. Thank you, Uncle Bobby."

Jenny took the cup and went to the porch swing. She sank down in the soft pillows and took a long sip. "It's something about being back here. The house and the land, everything is speaking to me, like voices. I was looking out across the fields and remembering my papa going off to work in the harvest... coming home to Mama and me..."

Bobby nodded. "I spent many happy hours in this house. Your mama was so beautiful and so delightful, so gifted. Your dad looked like a movie star and Jerusha was prettier than Grace Kelly. From the first moment I met her, she welcomed me into her heart."

"It was because my papa loved you, Uncle Bobby."

Bobby sat for a moment, blinked a few times, and then wiped his eyes with the edge of his sleeve. "I still have Reuben's CMH. He won it at the Battle of Bloody Ridge on Guadalcanal. I remember lying in the trench, looking up at Reuben as he defended our position single-handedly against a hundred Japanese soldiers. He got shot, stabbed, beat on... but he stayed there and kept them from going over the ridge. I wouldn't be alive except for your pop."

Jenny sighed deeply. "Do you ever long for the old days, Uncle Bobby?"

"Well, when you get to my age, and reflect on the past, you realize that all the 'old days' make you what you are. I've heard people say they would like to be twenty again but still know everything they learned getting to eighty. But then you wouldn't be who you are now, when you got to eighty the second time. Does that make sense?"

Jenny laughed. "Lots, I think." They both laughed.

"Now, last night, Uncle Bobby, I noticed Jarod left us a well-stocked refrigerator, so I say we go inside, roust my lazy daughter and her husband and get some Amish casserole cooking."

"Way ahead of you, Mama." Rachel's head peeked around the door. "Daniel and I have been doing the heavy lifting in the kitchen while you old folks sat out here reminiscing and enjoying the fall morning. Come on, breakfast is almost ready."

~

JENNY PLACED her mama's box on the table in the evidence room. Bobby and Elbert watched as she unhooked the straps and took the lid off. She lifted out different bundles of cloth samples Jerusha had saved over the years. There were different pieces of backing material, and large spools of thread. Jenny set them to one side and pulled out a leather case. It had a zipper that ran around three of the case's sides. Jenny unzipped it and laid it open on the table. There were scissors, other tools and packets of needles all strapped in neat rows on one side and spools of different colored threads on the other.

"This is my mama's travel case. She took this with her when she went to quilt with some of the other Amish women."

Finally, Jenny pulled out a thick eight-and-one-half by eleven-inch notebook. She opened it and turned to the first page.

"This book has ideas for designs and plans for different quilts. There should be a section for all the quilts she made."

Jenny leafed through a few pages. "Yes, the designs start here, with the Rose of Sharon quilt my mama made in memory of my little sister, Jenna."

Bobby nodded. "That was the quilt she was going to enter at the Dalton Quilt Faire, after Jenna died. She was going to use the prize money to leave Apple Creek forever. Instead, she used the quilt to keep the little girl she found in the heart of a blizzard warm."

Elbert looked at Bobby and then at Jenny. "Sounds like a real adventure. What happened?"

Jenny smiled. "The little girl she saved was me. She wrapped me in the quilt and kept me alive until Papa and Uncle Bobby found us. I still have the quilt."

Jenny went back to the book. The list of quilts was there, each one detailed in Jerusha's beautiful cursive script. The Aumans' quilt was there with all the design details and materials. Bernard Kauffman, Gerald Byler, Susan Wengard, all the families they had visited. Jenny went on down the list.

"There should be about six more... Let's see, here they are—Len Miller, Rebecca Hilty, Vernon Lambright, Thomas Beiler, Aaron Fisher... That's odd. I distinctly remember ten quilts."

Jenny looked at the list. "I think we can eliminate all but two of these. Mama was very specific about the design. It says here she made Lone Star quilts for the Troyers and the Fishers. We should check with them first."

Bobby took out a Camel and caught the sharp look from Elbert. "Right. No smoking in the evidence room. Sorry, Elbert." He slipped the cigarette back in the pack. "Do you remember where they all live, Jenny?"

"I remember where the Millers lived and I'm sure they or someone in the community can help us find the Fishers."

Elbert stood up. "Let's go check out the one you remember and see if they can help us."

∼

THE THREE INVESTIGATORS walked down the steps from the Miller's front porch. Len Miller walked with them.

"Sorry I couldn't help you, Jenny. Your mama's gift to us has become like an heirloom. We would never get rid of it or lose it."

Jenny shrugged. "It's all right, Len. I'm just glad that my mama meant so much to your family. And it's been really wonderful to see her quilts again."

They climbed into the car, Elbert and Bobby in the front. Elbert drove and Jenny sat in the back, alone. She was thinking about the quilts. Finally, she leaned forward and spoke to Bobby. "The Troyer's quilt was a Lone Star, but it was pink, not purple. The only one left is the one she made for the Fishers, at least according to the book. If they still have theirs, then I'm at a loss. I just..."

Bobby turned his head. "What, Jenny."

"I am almost positive that my mama made ten gift quilts. And four of them were Lone Stars. But it's not in the book and I'm wondering why."

∼

Later that night, Jenny sat in the kitchen alone with her mama's box. Bobby, Rachel, and Daniel were in bed. The day had been a long one, unproductive, and they had hit a dead end. After the Troyer family, they visited the Fishers. They also still had their quilt. And when they checked with the other three families, just in case one of them had the missing quilt, they had come up empty. So now Jenny was going through the box again. She pulled out everything, spread it out on the table, and began looking through it. Nothing. Then she took the book and leafed through it. She looked at the pages with the gift families on them. Again, there was nothing. She took the book by the spine and, holding the front and back covers spread open, she shook it. Nothing. She shook it one more time and a tiny, torn, piece of paper slipped out from between two of the pages.

Carefully, Jenny picked it up.

What's that doing in there?

Jenny went back to the quilt pages, laid the book flat on the table, and looked in between the pages. After the ninth quilt, she found what she was looking for. A page had been torn from the book and the stub was almost invisible. But there was a small piece that had not been torn out.

Mama wouldn't have torn a page out. Someone else tore it, but they did it quickly and didn't get the whole page.

She looked at the small piece that remained in the book.

... nice Johnson

A name! Somebody named Johnson.

Johnson is not an Amish name. Maybe she made the last quilt for an Englischer. But why? Mama never did that before.

Jenny stood up and stretched. She stared at the name once more and then gathered up the materials from the box, put it inside and closed the lid. She turned off the gas lamp and made her way to her bed.

SOMETIME IN THE middle of the night, Jenny fell into troubled dreams. She was lost in Jepson's woods, wandering in a damp and clinging mist. The trees and brush loomed on every side and it was cold, very cold.

The thought came to her... *As cold as the grave....*

She stumbled over something. When she looked down she saw a box, part way out of the ground. The lid was pushed aside and the box was empty. She heard a noise, rustling, like someone running through the woods. She peered into the mist. Ahead of her she saw something slipping through the trees, a figure, a flash of purple in the half-light. She called after it, "Wait, wait! You have to show me the answer..."

Through the trees she saw a light, and she knew that if she could just get to the light she would know the truth.

If only I can get to the light...

∽

EARLY IN THE MORNING, before sunrise, something awakened Jenny, a sound, not a normal sound, something that her ears heard because it was different. She sat up in bed. Then she heard another sound, the creak of a footfall in the hallway. She slipped from her bed and went to the door of her room. Suddenly there was a crash from the kitchen and light flooded under the door. She swung the door open to see Bobby moving swiftly down the hall with a drawn pistol. She followed him as he turned into the kitchen. In the kitchen, the back door was open, and she saw Daniel going out the door on the run. Something had shattered the kitchen window by the back door. Jenny looked at the table.

Her mama's box was gone!

8
LITTLE GIRL FOUND

*J*enny rushed to the table. Jerusha's box had vanished, along with everything in it. Jenny sank down at the table. "Why didn't I put it away? Oh, Mama..."

The back screen swung open and Daniel came in. He was out of breath. "Because you thought we were safe here. I'm sorry, Jenny. They got away..."

Jenny looked up. "What happened, Daniel?"

"I heard a noise in the kitchen and I came out. The back door was open and there was someone at the table. I grabbed the fry pan off the stove and threw it at them."

Daniel shrugged and pointed sheepishly at the shattered window.

"I missed..."

Bobby put the pistol on the table and sat down. "Could you tell if it was a man or a woman?"

Daniel shook his head. "It was dark. A scarf or something covered their face. I can tell you this, though. They were in pretty good shape, because they out-ran me and got into the woods. That's where I lost them. I'm sorry, Jenny."

Jenny put her face in her hands. "It's not your fault, Daniel. I should have taken the box to my room."

Bobby put his hand on Jenny's shoulder. "Was the notebook in the box?"

Jenny's hands muffled her answer. "Yes."

Then Jenny lifted her head. "Wait a minute... I found something last night."

Rachel had come in to the kitchen. "What did you find, Mama?"

"There was a page torn out of the book. But there was still part of the page left. And there was a name on it—Johnson."

"That's not an Amish name."

"That's right. And the last four letters of the first name were there, too.... n-i-c-e."

"That could be Bernice, or... or..."

"Eunice," Bobby said.

He looked around the table. "My wife's name was Eunice."

Jenny's mouth dropped open. "You were married, Uncle Bobby?"

Bobby smiled. "Yep. I was seventeen, and she was sixteen. She married me to get away from home. She wanted to move to Columbus. You know... bright lights, big city. I didn't want to go. So she did, and I didn't. And that was that."

"Uncle Bobby, I never knew that."

Bobby shrugged. "I never told many people. My folks knew, my sister knew, your pop knew. It was a short and forgettable episode in my life."

"But why didn't you ever get married again?"

"Right after she left, Pearl Harbor happened and your dad and I joined the Marines. After Cactus... uh, Guadalcanal... when I got home, I discovered I was pretty much set in my ways already, so I never pursued it. Seems to have worked out all right."

Jenny shook her head. "You know somebody for sixty years and you think you know everything about them..."

Bobby shrugged and grinned. "What can I say?"

Rachel pulled up a chair. "Listen, Mama. A thought just came to me. *Grossmütter* Jerusha was very meticulous. She wouldn't have torn a page out of her book unless there was something she didn't want people to see. And in the Amish community, especially Old Order Amish, what could cause real difficulty for someone?"

Daniel looked at his wife. "If you were breaking the ban and communicating with someone who was under the *meidung?*"

"Or making a quilt for an *Englischer...*"

"Or both. Maybe Jerusha made a quilt for someone that was under the ban or was not of our faith and then she worried about people finding out."

Jenny looked up. "Or maybe the person she made the quilt for asked Mama to take her name out of the book because she was afraid someone would find out and it would go hard with Mama."

Bobby looked around at the stove. Rachel grinned. "Want some *kaffee*, Uncle Bobby?"

Bobby nodded. Then he joined in the conversation. "Suppose the person your mama made the quilt for was an Amish girl who married outside the faith, say she married an *Englischer* named Johnson. That would really put her beyond the pale, so to speak. All we need to do is talk to someone who would know the goings on in the community back then."

Jenny nodded. "It seems like that's about all we've got to go on. It's worth a try."

∽

"Ja, I remember when that happened." Milt Auman leaned back in his chair and took a puff on his pipe. "It was quite a scandal, as I recall."

Jenny looked at Bobby and Elbert. Milt went on.

"Chantrice Stoltzfus, that was her name."

"Chantrice?"

"*Ja*. It's a French name. Her parents came over from Alsace-Lorraine before World War II. That's in France, you know. Chantrice was just a little girl then."

Jenny gasped. "Maybe it wasn't n-i-c-e. The letters could have been r-i-c-e. Go on Milt."

"Her folks were very... how shall I say it... very 'old country.' Very rigid in their ways. Old man Stoltzfus was a miller, and a good one. His mill did *sehr gut*, and he made a lot of money, so he was in with the *Bisschopf* and all that crowd. Well, when Chantrice was about sixteen, she fell in love with an *Englischer*. Let's see... yes. His name was Merrill, Merrill Johnson. He was a mill worker over at Moreland. She got... well, she got..."

Mrs. Auman piped up. "She got pregnant, that's what happened, and back then it was a real scandal. Her folks threw her out, and she got married to the Johnson boy and went to live with him. She had a little girl, I believe."

"Does she still live around here?"

"I don't know, Bobby. She dropped out of sight when all that happened. That's been almost sixty years ago."

Milt took another puff. "One thing I know, she was good friends with your mama, Jenny."

Jenny looked at Milt. "Chantrice knew my mama?"

"Yep. Jerusha was older, but she took Chantrice under her wing. She used to care for her because Mrs. Stoltzfus was not well and Henrí was at the mill a lot. The girls got very close, as close as two peas in a pod. Your mama was such a gentle soul, and she was like Chantrice's big sister. When all that kerfuffle with Chantrice happened, your mama was very upset. I'm sure the elders told Jerusha to keep away from Chantrice."

Mrs. Auman broke in again. "But knowing your mama, she would have at least let Chantrice know she loved her."

"... By making her a quilt." Jenny smiled. "Yes, that was my mama. And I know how all that feels because I got put under the *bann*."

Milt nodded. "*Ja*, I remember. Ran away with that *Englischer* fella from San Francisco... Caused quite a stir in Apple Creek back then."

Jenny blushed. "I know, and I was very sorry when I found out Jonathan was on the run from a bunch of crooks."

Mrs. Auman pushed in. "Well, all's well that ends well, Jenny Hershberger. Your Jonathan was Amish all along, wasn't he?"

Jenny nodded. "Yes, and not only that, but he was a Hershberger, and his roots were originally in the Northkill settlement in Pennsylvania. His great-great-grandfather left the faith, but he had a twin brother, Joshua Hershberger, who came to Apple Creek after the Revolutionary War and founded my mama's family."

Mrs. Auman shook her head. "Well, don't that beat all. And then you met Jonathan all those years later, and he had no idea about his family's past?"

Jenny smiled at the memory. "He was lost back in those days, but as soon as I showed him his roots, he fell in love with the Amish way. Before we got married, my Grandfather Borntraeger took him in and discipled him."

Elbert, who had been listening to all this, spoke up. "From what I've heard, Jenny, you've led a very exciting life. You should write a book."

Bobby laughed. "She did. Four of them—and she's working on two more."

Jenny blushed. "Let's not get into that, Uncle Bobby. I try to keep that under wraps. I'm kind of pushing the envelope with my elders as it is."

Milt looked at Jenny with a twinkle in his eye. "Oh, we know all about that, Jenny. How you write books, give the manuscripts to an *Englisch* author, and he publishes the books for you under his name. Not a lot of secrets in Apple Creek, you know."

Mrs. Auman got up and left the room. When she came back, she had a book. She handed it to Jenny.

Jenny looked at the cover.

A Quilt for Jenna.

Milt looked surprised. "Mama! I didn't know you had that book."

"Well, of course I have it, Milton! It's a wonderful story about Jerusha and our Jenny is a wonderful writer. Just because we are Amish doesn't mean we can't be talented."

She glanced over at Jenny. "Would you... would you sign it for me?"

Jenny blushed. "I don't know, Mrs. Auman. I would feel strange..."

"I promise you, Jenny, I will tell no one. It would mean so much to me. It's the story of your mama and we all loved her so much."

Jenny smiled. "Then, of course I will, Mrs. Auman." Jenny took the book. Mrs. Auman handed her a pen, and she wrote something brief on the flyleaf.

"Thank you so much, you darling girl. This book will go right with the quilt. It will be a treasure for our family."

Elbert scratched his head. "And here I thought I was just going to ask a few questions of a... of a..."

Jenny laughed. "... a doddering old Amish woman who didn't know what a telephone was, right, Detective?"

It was Elbert's turn to blush.

~

THREE DAYS LATER, Elbert, Bobby and Jenny sat in Elbert's office at the police station. Elbert was rustling through a sheaf of papers.

"We looked in the old records of Wayne County and found a marriage license for a Chantrice Stoltzfus and Merrill Johnson in 1951. But that's all we found. There's no address or any records.

We looked for a divorce. We traced all the Johnsons in Wayne County. Nothing."

Bobby looked at Elbert. "How about death records? Maybe one or both of them died."

Elbert nodded and picked up the phone. "Hey, Janice, I need you to search for me in the death certificates in Wayne County. See if anyone named Chantrice Stoltzfus, Chantrice Johnson or Merrill Johnson died from 1951 to 1970. Thanks."

Elbert hung up and looked over at Jenny and Bobby. "This is turning into quite a goose-chase. We are trying to find a woman who might have been mentioned in your mother's notes. A woman who left the Amish community in 1951. That's fifty-six years ago. And maybe it was her, but all we have is a briefly glimpsed little scrap with part of a name on it. And then if we find this… this Chantrice, we must connect her to a body that's been in the ground almost forty years. I don't know if this case is going anywhere. It just seems like too many variables."

Jenny nodded. "I understand what you are saying, Detective, but if my mama cared for Chantrice as much as the Aumans say she did, then it would have been very like her to make a quilt for her. So, if Chantrice was pregnant in 1951, the baby could be the girl who was found in the box. If she had been dead forty years when they found her, that would have made her around sixteen years old when she was killed."

Bobby agreed. "What we know is that Jerusha made the quilt, and when she was taking them around to people, Jenny was between eight and twelve years old. Do you remember taking a quilt to someone named Chantrice, Jenny?"

Jenny shook her head. "No, but then if my mama was being careful to keep it secret, she probably wouldn't have taken me along. I had a big mouth in those days. So Mama probably played it safe."

Just then, the phone on Elbert's desk rang. He picked it up.

"Yeah, Janice. Oh, really. Anything else? Wooster? Okay,

thanks." Elbert hung up the phone. "Janice found an internet record of a death certificate for Merrill Johnson. He was killed in a mill accident in Moreland in 1962. There was an article about it. Survived by Chantrice Johnson."

"That's our girl," said Jenny. "Any information about Chantrice?"

"Her last known address was an apartment in Wooster. We can go there tomorrow."

~

ELBERT WAINWRIGHT KNOCKED on the door of the small duplex in Wooster. Jenny and Bobby stood behind him. He waited and then knocked again. Finally, the door opened a crack.

"Yes, what is it?"

"Chantrice Johnson?"

The door opened a little wider and Jenny could see a seamed face with unkempt white hair framing it.

"I am Chantrice Edwards. Who are you and what do you want?"

"I'm detective Elbert Wainwright of the Wooster Police Department. Were you ever married to Merrill Johnson?"

"Yes, but that was long ago. I married again after Merrill died. What is this about?"

Elbert opened the folder and took out a picture. "Do you recognize this, Mrs. Edwards?"

There was a quick gasp, and then the door opened wider and the old woman reached out and took the picture. She stared at it for a long moment and then looked up at Elbert.

"Why... why, that's Emma's quilt."

9

EMMA

*J*enny stepped forward. "Do you remember me, Mrs. Edwards? I'm Jenny Hershberger, but my name used to be Jenny Springer."

A strange look came over Chantrice's face. "Jenny Springer? Jerusha Springer's daughter?"

"Yes, Mrs. Edwards, Jerusha's daughter."

"But what are you doing here? And why do you have a picture of that quilt?"

Elbert cleared his throat. "Can we come in, Mrs. Edwards? It's important that we ask you some questions."

Chantrice looked from Elbert to Jenny and then to Bobby. "I know you. You're Sheriff Halverson."

Bobby nodded. "That's right, ma'am. And we really need to speak with you."

Chantrice looked at Elbert again and then opened the door and stepped aside. "The house is a mess," she mumbled. "I wasn't expecting visitors."

They went inside. It was a tiny apartment with a kitchenette off the living room. In the back of the kitchen, the door leading to the bathroom was open. Another open door to the left led to a bedroom.

Stacks of old newspapers littered the coffee table by the couch. The room smelled stale, cigarettes and alcohol with a faint odor of vomit. Cigarette smoke had stained the top two feet of the wallpaper and the one window looking out on the street was unwashed and partially covered by faded chintz curtains. Overflowing ashtrays sat on every counter and table. Mrs. Edwards hurriedly picked some up and emptied them into a wastebasket. Then she motioned for them to sit down.

Jenny and Elbert sat on the couch. An old blanket covered it, and Jenny had to shift a bit when she felt a spring that had poked through the sofa cover. Chantrice dropped into an old lounge chair while Bobby grabbed a metal chair with a green plastic-covered seat and backrest from the kitchen dinette and pulled it into the living room.

"So, what do the police want with me? What's this all about?"

She paused. "Is this about Emma?"

Elbert spoke up. "Who's Emma, Mrs. Edwards?"

"My daughter. Something's happened to her, right?"

"We don't know yet. Is Emma here?"

Chantrice shook her head and chuckled. "Here? Not hardly. I haven't seen Emma for forty years." She looked at Elbert and frowned. "But that's her quilt you have a picture of. Where did you get it?"

Jenny leaned forward. "Mrs. Edwards, did you read about the girl they found buried in a box over in Apple Creek?"

Chantrice nodded. "I heard about that, yes."

"Well, the body was wrapped in the quilt in the picture."

Chantrice's mouth went open, and she looked from face to face. At last she spoke. "I knew it. I knew something bad happened to her. She may have been a bad girl, but she wouldn't have just gone away."

Bobby spoke up. "We don't know if there's a connection yet.

This is the first time that we have heard about Emma and we will need to have the pathologists make a positive identification. Did you have a dentist back then, one that Emma went to?"

Chantrice nodded.

"If you would give us permission, we would like to obtain Emma's dental records. Is there anything else that might have some DNA we could use?"

Chantrice wiped her eyes and went into her bedroom. In a moment, she came back with a box. "This is all I have. She didn't take it when she left."

Chantrice opened the box. Inside were some lipsticks, a hand mirror, and a hairbrush. Elbert quickly slipped on a latex glove and picked up the brush. Entwined in the bristles were several long red hairs. Nodding, he put the brush back in the box. "This will do very well. If the girl we found is your daughter, we will find out. In the meantime, don't give up hope."

Jenny leaned forward. "Mrs. Edwards, can I ask you about the quilt?"

Chantrice nodded.

"When did my mama give you the quilt?"

Chantrice concentrated for a moment. "I think it was about 1955. I married Merrill in 1951, and of course, the Amish people threw me out. All but your mama. She was always so kind to me. When we were in school, she… she looked after me. She was a lot older, but we just seemed to hit it off. She would come to my house and babysit me when my mama was having one of her… spells. Mama was never well and stayed in bed a lot."

Jenny nodded. "I used to help her deliver her gift quilts, but I don't remember bringing one to your house."

"I saw her in town one day and she said she wanted to bring me something. I told her not to come to see me. I begged her not to. My father had turned all the Amish against me and if they knew Jerusha broke the *bann*, he would have gotten them to shun her too. But she came anyway."

"When was that, Mrs. Edwards?"

Chantrice leaned over and put her hand on Jenny's arm. "Please, call me Chantrice." She thought again. "It was in the winter of 1955. Jerusha had gone through all that trouble with Jenna dying and then Reuben left, but then somehow everything turned out all right. Because of all the turmoil in Jerusha's life, I hadn't seen her except for that one time in the village. Late one night, there was a knock on my door. It was Jerusha. She had this beautiful quilt for me. Emma was four. I gave her the quilt, and it became her security blanket. Her... her father had been killed only a few months before."

"Merrill?"

Chantrice looked sharply at Jenny. "Yes! Merrill." She looked away, then spoke again.

"Emma was never without the quilt after that. When we went in the car, she took it. When she sat on the couch watching TV, she had it with her. It took me a long time to break her of her dependency. When she left home, she took her clothes and the quilt with her."

"When did she leave?"

"The summer of 1967. I thought she went out to San Francisco with her boyfriend—you know... that Summer of Love thing. Dennis talked about it all the time. Lots of drugs, great rock and roll bands. When she left, I knew that's where they went. But when I never heard from either of them again, after a while I felt like something bad had probably happened."

Elbert got out a pad. "What was her boyfriend's name?"

"Dennis, Dennis Cummings. He was a real loser, involved in drugs and all that. I'm sure he got Emma hooked on that stuff. She got very secretive before she left. I just knew she had gone bad. Somehow, I think I've always known something bad happened to her. It's been almost forty years. But I can't believe she was murdered right here in Apple Creek. No, it just can't be. If she's dead, she died out in California."

Jenny looked at Chantrice. "Let's hope you're right, Chantrice."

"Does Cummings have family around here?"

"No. He was a foster child. Never knew his folks."

Chantrice put her head down. "Poor Emma, my poor girl."

Jenny patted her arm. "Chantrice, we don't know yet if it's Emma..."

Chantrice shook her head. "Well, that was her quilt. Why would it end up wrapped around some other dead girl? Maybe it is Emma. But who in the world would want to hurt her right here in Apple Creek?"

Chantrice put her face in her hands and sat in silence.

∽

ELBERT SAT BEHIND HIS DESK. The afternoon sun was trying to heat the room, so he got up and turned the pole that adjusted the blinds to cut some of the light. Just then, the phone rang. He picked it up.

"Wainwright here. Oh hi, Doctor Stevens." He paused while the other person spoke. "What? The hairs didn't match? Well, that's a monkey wrench, for sure." Elbert hung up the phone, leaned back in his chair, and stared at the ceiling. Then he said to no one in particular, "And here I thought we had this thing all wrapped up."

Elbert looked down at the Sudoku puzzle he had been working on and then dropped the pencil with a sigh. The intercom sounded. He flicked the switch. "Yeah, what?"

"It's Jenny Hershberger and Sheriff Halverson."

"Okay, Janice, send them in."

In a few moments, Bobby and Jenny walked in. Elbert looked up.

"How did you do?"

Bobby nodded. "The office Chantrice told us about has been

closed for about five years—a Doctor Garner. We asked the neighboring businesses, and one person—the owner of a hardware store across the street—knew the doctor and gave me an address. I'll look him up. We will need to find out if there are any records for Emma. It's going to take some research."

Elbert frowned. "Well, I got some bad news. The hairs on the brush didn't match the victim's hair."

Jenny looked at Bobby in surprise. Then she shook her head. "Well, that's not surprising."

"What do you mean?"

"It's just that I've learned that as far as this case is concerned, nothing is ever simple." Jenny sat in the chair across from Elbert. "So, what's our next step, Detective?"

Elbert folded up the newspaper with the Sudoku puzzle and slipped it into a drawer. "Well, we are kind of at a dead end. We have a suspect before we know who the victim is. That's backwards. Whoever broke into your house is obviously number one on our suspect list and knows who the victim is, but we do not know who that suspect is, nor do we have the knowledge our suspect has. Namely, he knows who he killed and we don't."

Bobby shook his head. "I don't know, detective. If the guy who tried to steal the box at the train station is the same person who broke into the house, then it can't be him. He wasn't over twenty years old."

Jenny spoke again. "Here's what I think. We have a dead girl in a box, we have a girl who's been missing the same amount of time as the victim has been dead, and we have a powerful connection between the missing girl, the dead girl and the quilt. If the victim wasn't Emma, it's someone who knew Emma—someone close enough that she would end up with the quilt. So, I think we just keep going on this track."

Bobby pulled out his Camels. "Okay if I smoke?"

Elbert nodded his assent.

Bobby lit up and took a drag. "Jenny's right. We keep going as though Emma is the victim. That makes the boyfriend a real person of interest."

Jenny took out a notepad from her bag. "Chantrice said Dennis Cummings was a foster child. Maybe we can find some records through the Foster Care Service. We can start there."

"Jenny's right. We also need to find the dentist, we need to visit the mother again and we need to go over all the evidence you have here with a fine-tooth comb."

Jenny nodded. "And what about the phone call I got? Was that Dennis Cummings, or our break-in guy or somebody else entirely? Maybe it was just someone Amish who is concerned about all the publicity and the focus on their community."

Bobby took another drag. "And we can't limit ourselves to one suspect. Some cases have the most surprising perps. And most murders center on sex or money. So, even before we verify that we have Emma, we need to go back to her mother and get every bit of information we can. There may be some not so obvious players."

Bobby looked over at Jenny, who was chewing thoughtfully on the end of her pencil. "What's on your mind, Jenny?"

Jenny shook her head. "I don't know. There's something not right about all this, but I can't put my finger on it. I think Chantrice knows more than she's saying. We definitely need to go see her again."

10

GO BACK TO THE BEGINNING

*J*enny sat in the kitchen at the old Apple Creek house. She pondered the case of the girl in the quilt.

Mama used to tell me that the goings on in a small village and the people involved in those goings-on were a perfect microcosm of the world around that village. And that if you could just watch the everyday people around you, it would tell you a lot about human nature.

Jenny got up and went to her room. When she returned, she had two large folders. She put them down on the table and returned to her seat in the chair. The folders were both titled 'Dear Jenny Articles/Letters.' One was dated 1985-1994 and the second 1995-2005. She opened the first one and looked through the stacks of typewritten sheets.

This case reminds me of what happened to Jeremy King, my publisher friend who the church put under the bann because a bisschopf lied about him. The people in Lancaster all believed the bisschopf and Jeremy had to leave town. It turned out that the bisschopf was a crook...

"Samuel Lapp..."

Just then, Rachel came into the kitchen. "Who?"

"Samuel Lapp. Don't you remember? He was the *bisschopf* who caused my parents' deaths."

Rachel nodded. "Oh, yes, such a nasty little man. Isn't he still in prison?"

"Yes. He was also involved in extortion and fraud over in Pennsylvania, so they gave him a big sentence here, and then took him to Lancaster and he got more there. He was a real... a real *schweinhund!*"

Rachel's mouth dropped open. "Mama!"

Jenny blushed. "Sorry, Rachel, but I still harbor bad feelings toward the man. I've tried to forgive him many times... but..." Jenny looked up. "I guess it's something *Gott* will have to help me work out." She sighed. "But it's hard."

There was a moment of silence, and then Rachel switched directions. "Why were you thinking about him?"

Jenny took a deep breath. "Well, I was just sitting here remembering what my mama used to tell me about human nature. All the things that go on in a small village will give you great insight about people anywhere in the world and why they all do the same kinds of things. And I was thinking that the Amish community is not the peachy-keen, perfect world that most people think it is, especially those *Englischers* who buy those 'Amish fiction' books off the shelf at Walmart. Amish fiction, indeed!"

Rachel nodded. "Fiction. *Ja,* you can say that again. My story is proof of that. At one point I was one of the wealthiest people on the planet... that is until I found out that the man who was supposed to be managing the St. Clair trust fund had looted every penny, and the people I trusted were trying to kill me. Not exactly a light-hearted happily-ever-after Amish romance like you read in those little cookie-cutter books."

"And that's what I'm talking about. After they bandied your story about the Amish community in Paradise for several months, and after *The Amish Heiress* was published, one of those *Englisch* authors who write about us all the time put out a book called '*The Amish Millionaire.*' But it certainly didn't talk about any desperate situations in the Amish community. No. The worst thing that happens in those books is when the wheel falls off the *bisschopf's* son's buggy on his way to court the gorgeous Amish princess."

They both laughed. Jenny went on. "Here's my point. Most criminals commit crimes in the place where they live, among their own community. And the Amish community is no different. We have crime, we have hatred, we even have murder. So just because we are Amish doesn't mean we don't have wicked people right in our midst. Samuel Lapp blackmailed people, stole their land, got his enemies excommunicated... hurt my parents..."

Rachel leaned over and hugged her mama. Jenny took out a hanky and wiped her eyes. Then she went on.

"I guess my point is Chantrice is Amish, even though she's been shunned for fifty years. So Chantrice is connected to the Amish in her heart for good or bad. It's in her blood. Just like me. You can't deny who *Gott* created you to be."

Rachel nodded. "Tell me about it. I certainly tried to not be Amish when I married Gerald St. Clair and went off to live the life of the rich and famous. Nothing I did could make me anything but who I was. I thank *du lieber Gott* that Daniel was around to love me and point me in the right direction. So what you're saying is..."

"... Emma's murder is tied in to the Amish community, because the entire story started right here in Apple Creek. I don't think we have to go outside the village to find out who put Emma in the box."

"If it is Emma who they buried in the box."

"Oh, it's Emma, all right, I just know it is. Look. Emma has a favorite quilt that my mama made for her. From the time she is five years old, she is never without it. Then when she's seventeen, she packs up and leaves and no one ever hears from her again.

Forty years later, a girl that would have been Emma's age when she was killed, turns up in a box wrapped in Emma's security blanket. The girl in the box has to be Emma."

"But the hair didn't match."

"Look at it the other way. Maybe Emma's hair didn't match the hair on the brush. If the conclusion doesn't fit, go back to your premise. So, if it didn't match, what does that tell you? What's the wrong assumption?"

"We assumed the hair on the brush is Emma's hair?"

"Exactly, Rachel. So, if the hair on the brush is not Emma's hair, then either someone else used the brush, or somebody put different hair on the brush..."

"... to misdirect us... or push us in a different direction."

Jenny smiled while Rachel got the coffee pot and poured them both a cup. "You know, Mama, that's exactly what I told Daniel. Somebody who knows you, or knows about you—how you're a historian, how you know all about the Amish community and history, and how *zäh* you are—someone who knows about you is trying to scare you off or at least lead you away from the truth."

"Exactly, Rachel. How did they know to go after my mama's box unless they knew she kept everything about her quilts—meticulous records—in that box? It was someone who knew my mama, or was told about my mama's box by someone who knew her. And that brings our focus right back—"

Rachel nodded. "—to the Amish community of Apple Creek."

Jenny pulled a sheaf of paper from the folder.

"I used to get a lot of letters from people in various Amish communities, asking how I would handle some strange situation or another—things that have happened that no one could explain."

She shuffled through. "Here's one. A lady wrote to me about buying some chicken at the market. She shopped at a few more shops that day, but when she got home, she did not have the chicken."

Rachel looked sideways at her mama. "And that has to do with this case in what way?"

Jenny chuckled. "It has everything to do with it. The lady couldn't for the life of her figure out what she had done with the chicken. If she hadn't had the receipt for it, she would have thought she just imagined she bought it. Well, she sent me a note later. A neighbor came to tell her that when she left the store, she left the chicken on the counter. The neighbor saw another woman slip the chicken into her own bag and leave the store. It turns out that the thief was the lady's best friend."

"Which tells us...?"

"We know people commit crimes in their own communities, usually for one of three reasons—sex, greed, or anger. And people who are known in the community usually commit those crimes, even known to us. Like the lady's friend who knowingly stole her chicken, the perpetrator can be someone we would never suspect."

Rachel took a sip of her coffee. "I see. So, we may be looking for someone who is right in front of us, someone that knew Emma and knew you."

"Yes, that's right. So right now, we are looking at a murder where the assumption is somebody randomly killed this girl and then took the time to bury her in the heart of Jepson's woods in a box they got from somewhere at the time of the crime. Or a drugged out boyfriend who's been missing for forty years, too. Doesn't it seem more likely that this was a person who already had the box, killed the girl and then went to great lengths to make sure nobody ever found Emma? Why would they go to all that trouble if they didn't know Emma and they were just passing through? Or even if it was Dennis, where did he get the box, and why go to such lengths if it was a crime of passion?"

Rachel nodded agreement. "Exactly. If the killer was just

passing through or if it was somebody who got scared and ran away, they probably would have left the body in the woods or in a hastily dug grave close to the road they took going out of town."

"Exactly. Why hide the deed so thoroughly if you're never coming back to the scene of the crime?"

Just then, Bobby walked in. "Morning, ladies. What's up?"

Quickly, Jenny went over their discussion with Bobby. He listened attentively and then asked a question.

"So what does all this that tell us? I think you are right on, but my question is, what do we do about it?"

"What do you suggest, Uncle Bobby?"

"Like you said, if the assumption is wrong, go back to the premise. I think we need to look at everything the police have, even the body. There is something we missed there. We need to get everything we can find out about Emma from Chantrice—pictures, documents, letters, diary—everything. And just to make sure we get it all, we better get a search warrant."

11

THE RING

The next morning, Bobby and Jenny walked into the Wayne County Coroner's Office with Elbert. A girl behind the counter looked up and smiled.

"Hello, Detective. How can I help?"

"We need to see the girl in the box, Carol."

"Sure, I'll let Matt know you're coming in. He'll meet you down the hall."

She pressed something on her desk, and the metal door into the back of the building buzzed. Elbert pushed through, and Bobby and Jenny followed. At the end of the hall, they saw the coroner.

"Hey, Elbert."

"Matt."

"Here to see the girl in the box?"

"Yes, we are." He turned to Bobby and Jenny. "This is Jenny Hershberger and Bobby Halverson."

Matt stepped forward. "I know Bobby. How are you, Sheriff?"

"Fine, Matt. You've come a piece since I last saw you."

"Yes, I was just a grunt on the bottom of the food chain around here."

Bobby grinned. "Well, congrats."

"Thanks, Bobby. Mrs. Hershberger? I don't believe we've met."

Matt's words gave Jenny a little shock. Nobody but Elbert had called her Mrs. Hershberger for a long time. It made her think of Jonathan. She wondered what Jonathan would think of her new calling as an Amish detective. Being called Mrs. Hershberger brought a memory...

The day I met Jonathan. I was walking to the Library in Wooster...

Lost in her thoughts, Jenny came to the corner of Liberty and Walnut. She stepped off the curb without even stopping. She didn't see the vehicle making a left turn onto Walnut Street from Liberty. The driver honked his horn and swerved to avoid her, and the van screeched to a halt as it rammed one of its tires into the curb. The driver leaned out the window and yelled at her. "Hey, watch where you're going! I almost hit you."

"Well, if I remember correctly, pedestrians have the right of way!" Jenny called back.

"Yeah, they do if the light is in their favor," he said, pointing toward the signal.

Jenny looked back at the light. The left turn arrow was green, but the pedestrian light still said WAIT. *She felt herself wanting to say something nasty, but realizing she was in the wrong, she mumbled, "I'm sorry, I wasn't paying attention," and walked on.*

The young man behind the wheel called out to her. "Wait a minute, are you okay? I guess I should have been more careful..."

He opened the door and got out. Jenny stopped and looked back. "I'm fine. A little startled, but fine."

For the first time, Jenny looked at the driver. He was tall and trim, and his long hair was pulled back into a ponytail. He wore a leather jacket with fringe hanging down, bell-bottom jeans and green suede boots. Then she saw he was driving a blue Volkswagen van covered with strange pictures pasted on the van in a collage. There were flowers and strange foreign-looking men in very awkward positions.

The largest picture was on the driver's door. It was of a white-haired man in a white jacket with the words "Turn on, tune in, drop out" written below it. She looked back at the young man. She realized he was very good looking, but his most striking feature was his eyes. They were deep sea-blue, and she could see a hint of a smile behind them. She felt herself drawn into those eyes and had to pull herself back with a start.

His eyes—they are just like Papa's!

Jenny noticed that the young man was staring at her kappe. His eyes traveled down, taking in her face, and then her plain wool coat with the hooks instead of a zipper, and then the high-top laced shoes.

"Excuse me," he said. "Are you in a play or something?"

"What?" Jenny asked.

"A play," he said. "You're dressed like you're in a play."

"Right," Jenny retorted, feeling both a blush and an irritation rising within her. "I'm one of the starving pilgrims and you must be Squanto, the Indian who saves us. But wait! The Indians didn't wear green suede boots or drive decorated trucks, so you must be one of those beatniks I've heard about. But I don't remember any beatniks at the first Thanksgiving, so I guess you're not in the play after all."

The young man smiled. "Whoa! Slow down! Beatniks dress in black and play bongos. I guess I'm what you folks would call a hippie, but in San Francisco, I felt a little more local. Right this minute, I feel about as local as a fish in a tree..."

I was so snarky to him.

Jenny smiled to herself.

"Mrs. Hershberger?"

Jenny came back with a start. "Oh, I'm sorry. It's just that no one has called me Mrs. Hershberger for a long time. It made me remember something..."

She took a deep breath and shook his hand "No, we haven't met... Matt?"

The coroner nodded and smiled.

Jenny went on. "You are probably wondering why an old Amish woman is looking at dead bodies. I'm involved in this case because the quilt your victim was wrapped in is a quilt my mother made about forty-five years ago."

"Really! That's very interesting, Mrs. Hershberger."

Another twinge. "Jenny, please."

"Sorry... Jenny. How did you come to discover this?"

"My mama was a prolific quilter and a master at the craft. She made four or five quilts a year along with all the other things she did, running an Amish household for my papa. Some quilts she made were gifts for people who were struggling, or just needed to know that someone cared. She 'signed' the quilts by putting a tiny heart on each one. Elbert showed me the quilt, thinking I might know something about it. I recognized the quilt when I saw it, and the heart confirmed it. My mama made it."

"Were you able to track down the person she gave this quilt to?"

"Yes, she gave it to a woman named Chantrice Johnson. At least that was her name at the time. Chantrice gave it to her little girl, Emma, and Emma was never without that quilt. When Emma disappeared about forty years ago, the quilt vanished, too. That's why we believe the girl you have is Emma Johnson."

Bobby interjected. "We tracked down the dentist who cared for Emma, but his office has been closed for a while. I got an address over toward Dalton from the hardware store that was across the street to check out, and I'll be doing that today. If we can get some dental records to match our victim, maybe we can make a positive ID."

Matt nodded and then turned and opened a large metal door with a window in it. They had to step through some hanging vinyl sheets, similar to those found in a walk-in freezer. The room they entered was large and modern, with several examination tables on wheels... and chilly.

"We have to keep it cool in here for obvious reasons, although in this victim's case, it doesn't really matter."

All around the room were large metal drawers with pull handles. Matt stepped up to one and pulled it open. There was a body under a white sheet. When Matt pulled it back, Jenny gasped. She had seen dead bodies before, but they were in a simple coffin in an Amish living room and they had been dead less than three days. This body was ghastly. The skull had a few pieces of hair clinging to a desiccated scalp. The mouth was gaping open, and the lips had drawn back in a macabre grin. Some of the rest of the skin on the body was missing, but much of it was mummified.

Jenny looked at Matt. "Why is some of the skin dry and some has vanished?"

Matt smiled. "The box was very well made and when they nailed it shut, it formed a fairly airtight barrier. My lab determined that the wood was mahogany and very dense. The ground the box was buried in was not down in the swampy area by the pond. It was located up on a small hill with good drainage."

"So a lot of moisture didn't get into the box, and rather than rotting, the flesh dried out?"

Matt nodded assent. "Exactly. So what you see is a body that has been mummified, or at least partly mummified, rather than rotting."

Jenny looked down at the body again. It was drawn up in a fetal position, knees up about chest level with the hands and arms compressed between the knees and the sternum, almost as if the body was praying.

Matt noticed Jenny's puzzled look and responded. "The box was only about four feet long, so in order to get the body inside, the perp had to fold the body up. Then, of course, it stiffened in that position."

Jenny had a thought. "Can we see the hands?"

Matt nodded. "I was going to cut the tendons today and lay

the body out so we could see if there were any other wounds besides the fractured skull... for the final coroner's report. If you want to observe, I can do that now."

Jenny's stomach was queasy, but she nodded yes.

Matt rolled a metal table over to the drawer and, after folding the thin rubber blanket beneath the body around the corpse, he lifted it onto the table and pushed it over under a row of hanging ceiling lights. Jenny, Bobby and Elbert followed along.

Matt opened a small plastic box that was attached to the side of the table. Inside was a row of various instruments in holders. He took a very sharp scalpel and gently cut the tendons that locked the knees in position. One by one, he stretched the legs out on the table, then rolled the body over on its back. Then he lifted the elbows and deftly cut the tendons. The arms loosened, and he straightened them out beside the hip bones.

Jenny looked down. There was something on the ring finger of the left hand.

"What's that?" She pointed.

Matt leaned over and looked closer. "It looks like a ring."

He gently lifted the hand and freed the ring from the finger. "It's gold. There's some material from the decayed skin, but the gold itself is untarnished. I couldn't see it before because the knees hid the hands. Good thing you came today. I might have missed it."

"May I see it?"

"Let me clean it up first, Mrs...."

"Just Jenny is fine, Matt."

"Right. Jenny! Give me a few minutes, and I'll clean the residue off."

Matt left the room for a few minutes and when he returned, he had the ring in a glassine bag. He put it down on the table under the lights. The debris was gone, and the ring shone with a dull golden color. "This is high quality gold, that's for sure. And there was an inscription inside. Go ahead and look. Here, use these." He handed Jenny a pair of latex examination gloves and a magnifying glass.

Jenny slipped them on and then removed the ring from the bag. She lifted it to the light and turned it so she could look inside. The glass enlarged the writing and made it very clear. Inscribed there were two words, both German.

Ewige Liebe

Jenny looked up at Bobby and Elwood. "It is German. It says 'Eternal Love'." Jenny looked back down at the body. "If this girl is Emma, and I'm very sure that she is, she was wearing a ring with a German inscription when she died. Emma was not Amish, but there's certainly enough Amish around to make German a familiar language. We need to visit Chantrice and ask about this ring. If Emma didn't own such a ring when she disappeared, then someone who expresses themselves passionately in German, someone who probably cared deeply for Emma, gave it to her before she was killed. And that person was most likely Amish."

12
MORE CLUES

"No, I never knew about a ring and I never saw her wearing one." Chantrice Edwards took a long pull on her Marlboro. "Where did you find this ring?"

Jenny brushed the smoke away from her face and rearranged herself on the couch. Elbert was in a chair across from them.

"Is this cigarette bothering you, Jenny? I'll put it out."

Jenny smiled. "Actually, yes, Chantrice, it is." Jenny smiled again as Chantrice stubbed out her smoke. "The ring was on the girl's finger. The position of the arms and legs hid it."

Chantrice looked at the picture Jenny had given her, then looked up. "You say it's gold?"

Elbert nodded. "Almost pure gold. It would have been very expensive even then."

"Well, her deadbeat boyfriend, Dennis, would never have had the money to buy it. She must have stolen it. Maybe Dennis killed her for it... that is, if it is Emma."

Elbert looked puzzled. "If he killed her for it, why wouldn't Dennis have taken it, then?"

Chantrice looked around for her cigarette and then saw the stub still smoking in the ashtray. She pulled her hand back.

"Right, of course. Well, since we don't even know if this is Emma, we couldn't possibly know where this person got it."

Jenny glanced over at Elbert. He had an interesting look on his face. He spoke up. "Mrs. Edwards, do you have any more personal effects or pictures that belonged to Emma?"

Chantrice shook her head. "Not that I know of, Detective. I'm pretty sure I gave you everything."

"Are you sure, Mrs. Edwards? There must have been more than just a small box with a hairbrush and some lipstick. School pictures, notebooks, a dairy...?"

Chantrice rubbed her hands together. "I moved a few times, and I lost a lot of my stuff. There may be a box somewhere. I'll have to look for it."

"That would be most helpful." He held out his card.

Chantrice waved it off. "Thanks, I have one. If I find anything, I'll call you."

Elbert stood. "Jenny, if you don't have anymore questions, I think we should go. I want to see how Bobby's doing."

Jenny stood up and put her hand on Chantrice's arm. "Chantrice, I know this is hard, but I truly believe the girl in the box is Emma. We will do our best to find out."

Chantrice shook her head. "I don't know how you can, Jenny. It's been so long, and there's really no way to identify the body."

"We are not done yet. We'll find out who that girl is."

~

BOBBY HALVERSON DROVE down Highway 250 until he reached Kidron Road. He turned left and headed toward Dalton. After a few minutes, he slowed down and pulled over. He got out of the car and walked across the road. There was a steep bank there on the other side. Not much had changed in sixty years.

It was right here in the big storm of 1950 that I found Henry Lowenstein's car. He hit a cow and swerved off the road. Crashed into that bank and blew his tires. Then he left Jerusha here and tried to walk out to get help. That windblown branch caught him in the temple down at Mark's place. Poor kid was out for two days.

Bobby thought about Jerusha and Reuben, the two best friends he ever had. He sighed and pulled the pack of Camels from his pocket. He looked at them.

One of these days, these hummers might just kill me. But so far, so good.

He lit one up and then pulled the piece of paper out.

2200 Kidron Road. Can't be more than a hundred yards from here.

Bobby got back in the car and drove slowly on. Sure enough, in about a hundred feet, he saw the mailbox, 2200 Kidron Road. Bobby turned the old Ford truck off the road and drove up the long driveway to the house. It was set amidst some Buckeye trees with a small green lawn in the front. The house was simple, made of brick, with a bed for flowers lining the front, starting from the concrete steps and running down to the left corner. Bobby got out of the truck and headed for the front steps. Before he got there, the screen door opened and a man stepped out. He was older, with white hair and a well-trimmed short white beard. His face was round and friendly and he wore slacks and a white shirt with a dark blue button-up argyle sweater.

"Sheriff Halverson?"

Bobby stuck out his hand. "Doctor Garner?"

The man shook Bobby's hand and smiled. "That's me. C'mon inside."

They made their way into the house. It was cozy inside, with a very lived-in feeling. A large comfortable-looking couch sat against one wall, with an antique leather-topped coffee table in front of it. A spinet piano stood against one wall with a couple of African Violets sitting on top of it. There was a piece of music opened on the piano and a picture of a lovely older woman next to the flowers.

Bobby glanced at the sheet music. *Liebestraum,* by Franz Liszt.

"That's my wife, Becky," the doctor said, pointing to the picture, "and that's her favorite piano piece. She was quite a brilliant pianist."

"Was?" said Bobby.

"Yes, she died three years ago."

"Oh, I'm sorry."

The doctor shook his head. "We had a wonderful life. She was my best friend for forty-five years. When she got sick, she never let it get her down. She stayed upbeat until the end. The day before she died, she sat at that piano and played me our song one more time."

Doctor Garner turned away and looked out the window. Outside it was an Apple Creek fall day. The buckeye trees were sporting crimson and gold. The sky was blue with flecks of clouds scattered across it, like a painter had shaken his brush on it. Dr. Garner stood there for a moment.

"She loved the fall."

Bobby waited until the doctor turned around. He smiled. "Forgive me, I get caught up sometimes."

"Sorry to bring up old memories."

The doctor shook his head and smiled. "Actually, Sheriff, they are the best things I have left. Now, can I get you some coffee?"

"Sure, I'd love a cup."

"Cream?"

"Nope. Black is fine."

"Military?"

"Marines. How did you know?"

"Most of the military guys I know drink their coffee black."

"Probably because we had no cream out there on Guadalcanal."

They both laughed. The doctor went out to the kitchen and returned with two mugs. Bobby took his gratefully. The doctor motioned him to the dining room table. "So, sit and tell me what's on your mind."

"Emma Johnson."

The doctor looked up from his cup. "Emma? She's been gone for forty years. Ran away, I heard."

"She was your patient?"

"Yes, I treated Emma from the time she was a little girl."

"You've heard about the girl in the box?"

Doctor Garner shook his head. "Yes, terrible..." He paused. "You don't think the girl is Emma Johnson, do you?"

Bobby shook his head. "We have excellent reason to believe it is. Somebody wrapped the body in a quilt that was given to Emma's mother, and Emma had it with her all the time. She was never without it, so..."

The doctor nodded. "The body in the box is most likely the girl who was never without the quilt the body was wrapped in."

"Yep."

"Well... actually, I'm not surprised if it is Emma."

"What makes you say that, Doc?"

"Emma was an unhappy little girl. Her mother was... how do I put this? Overbearing? Controlling?"

Bobby reached for his Camels, then pulled back his hand. Doctor Garner smiled.

"Hey, Gyrene, the smoking lamp is lit." He looked around and found an ashtray on a shelf, put it in front of Bobby. "My wife didn't like cigarettes, but I got the habit when I was in the service. So now I have a smoke every once in a while."

Bobby offered him one, and the doctor took it. Bobby lit him up. "Were you a Marine?"

"Yep, 1st Marines, Medical Battalion."

"You see action?"

"I got into the show late. Finished medical school in 1944 and enlisted. I got an officer's commission and landed on Okinawa with the 1st Div. That was something. You?"

Bobby lit a Camel. "I got my ticket home at the Battle of

Henderson Field. Shot three times, carried a piece of shrapnel in my hip for forty years."

"Well, I think that calls for a libation."

The doctor went to a cupboard near the table and pulled out a bottle. He poured two shots and handed one to Bobby.

"Semper fi, mac."

"Semper fi, Doc."

They finished their drink, and the doctor put his glass down. "I suppose you are looking for Emma's dental records?"

"Yes, if we had them we could at least find out if Emma is our girl."

Doctor Garner shook his head. "I have bad news for you, Sheriff."

"What's that, Doctor?"

"When I retired, I moved all my records into a storage room. They were there for years until..."

"Until?"

"Until last week when the storage place burnt down. They are pretty sure it was arson because they found an empty gas can in the field out back."

"Everything gone?"

"Yes, Sheriff, all my records. It seems the fire started right outside my unit."

Bobby shook his head. "And that would be right after they found the girl in the box?"

"Seems so, Sheriff."

Bobby took a drag and looked at the doctor. "Someone didn't want us to identify Emma by her dental records."

"It seems that way, doesn't it?"

Bobby finished his smoke and crushed it out. "Well, that's another dead end. Seems like there is someone in Apple creek who would just as soon we didn't find out who our mystery girl is." He stood up. "Doc, it's been nice meeting you."

"Hey, anytime you want to drop by and share a Blue Ribbon, you're more than welcome."

Bobby smiled. "I'll be calling you. Thanks, Doc."

∼

Elbert sat at his desk, tapping a pencil rhythmically and thinking. There was a knock on the door and his secretary stuck her head in. "Sheriff Halverson is here."

"Send him in."

Bobby walked in and sat in the chair Elbert pointed to. "So, find anything?"

Bobby shook his head. "It seems the doctor's records got burned up in an arson fire the day after they found the girl."

"That's odd, Bobby. But it tells us that someone who is very local is trying to keep us from finding out who this girl is. Otherwise, they wouldn't have known where the doctor kept his files."

"Unless it's just coincidence..."

"Now, Sheriff, you've been around this business long enough to know that there are never any coincidences in a case like this."

Bobby nodded. "I was just thinking, but you're right. If the doctor's records burnt up the day after they found the body, it's like putting up a red flag." Bobby looked out the window. "You got anything?"

"I want to see if we can get a rundown on this Dennis Cummings, the boyfriend. Chantrice seemed to think he and Emma might have been heading for San Francisco. Maybe they got drugged up. Dennis kills her and heads for the coast. Don't know how we could track him, but I can always send out an APB to police and sheriff's departments between here and San Francisco. We might get lucky."

"Well, I'm going to look up Jenny and go get something to eat. Want to join us?"

"No, thanks. I think I'll make some calls and send out some inquiries."

"Well, if you get hungry, we'll be over at Fishers."

"Okay, maybe I'll see you there."

Bobby got up to go. "Seems like we're beating a dead horse here."

Elbert shrugged. "Maybe, but I'm at least half an optimist. Something could turn up."

13

THE TOOTH FAIRY

"Dead ends."

"What?" Jenny looked up from her menu and glanced over at Bobby. "What did you say? I was looking at this deep-dish cherry pie."

Bobby grinned. "Dead ends. It seems like every time we get close to digging something up, we hit the wall. I'm thinking this girl is going into a pauper's grave with a headstone that says 'Jane Doe, ????—1967.' And don't you think you should have some dinner before desert?"

"I know. But the picture..."

Just then Geraldine Fisher scooted up. "You ready to order?"

Jenny nodded. "I want the pork chops and rice, but..."

Geraldine looked down at Jenny over the glasses perched on the end of her nose. "Yes?"

"Only if you can promise me there will be an enormous piece of the deep-dish cherry pie left by the time we finish."

Geraldine made a note on her pad. "I'll set it aside soon as I get back to the kitchen."

"Make that two pieces, Geraldine."

Mrs. Fisher shifted her gaze to Bobby. "You gonna have dinner first, Sheriff?"

Bobby nodded vigorously. "Yep. That corned beef and cabbage sounds mighty, mighty good."

"Corned beef it is, and the pork chops for Jenny. Anything else?"

"Couple mugs of coffee?"

"You got it. Cream?"

Bobby shook his head, but Jenny nodded yes. Geraldine went off to the kitchen to put in the order.

"So, what have we got?"

Jenny pulled out a small top-bound spiral notepad and flipped the pages until she came to what she wanted. "Okay... we have a dentist who could probably identify the body with dental records, only the records got burned up in a mysterious fire. We have a young man who tried to rob us at the train station and got away with Mama's book out the kitchen door the next day. The hair on Emma's brush doesn't match the corpse. The wooden box looks like Amish handiwork, and we have a gold ring buried with the girl. Not a lot."

"And we have the quilt."

Jenny nodded. "Yes, we have Mama's quilt and that's why I'm absolutely certain this is Emma Johnson. But how to prove that is beyond me."

Geraldine bustled up with the coffee. "Dinner will be right out and the cherry pie is warming. I'm assuming you'll be wanting some hand-churned vanilla ice cream on top of that?"

Both heads went up and down.

∼

LATER, as they leaned back in their chairs and Bobby tried to get the last little crumb of crust with the back of his fork, Jenny sighed. "You're the policeman, Bobby. What do you suggest?"

Bobby pulled out a Camel, glanced at Jenny, then laid it on the table. "Okay. The box looks like it is Amish made, most likely from somewhere close by. We need to have some photos taken from every angle and I need to visit all the antique stores and woodworkers in the county until I find someone who can tell me who made the box. Then there is the ring. You have better eyes than me so you need to go over it with a magnifying glass. It's an expensive ring, no cheap knock-off, so there just might be a jeweler's mark on it. We need to talk to Chantrice again. She seems very reluctant to believe this is Emma, and she should have more of Emma's things than just a box with a brush and some makeup. And that's what I got."

Just then the front door of the restaurant opened and a man walked in. He glanced around, saw Bobby, and came over. It was Doctor Garner. Bobby glanced up and then looked again. "Hey, Doc! What's up?"

The doctor looked around the restaurant quickly. "May I sit down?"

"Of course." Bobby stood and pulled a chair for the doctor. "Doc, this is Jenny Hershberger. She and I go way back in Apple Creek. Her parents were Reuben and Jerusha Springer."

"Sure, I knew the Springers. Swell folks. Was a terrible thing, that wreck and everything..."

To Jenny's surprise, she felt a lump come to her throat. Doctor Garner saw the momentary look of distress and put his hand on Jenny's arm. "I'm sorry. I should keep my mouth shut."

"No, it's very kind of you to remember them to me. I'm fine. It was a long time ago..."

Bobby broke in. "What brings you here, Doc?"

The doctor whispered. "I was looking for you and the man at the motel said you were probably here. Something has come up, but I don't want it getting around because we know someone has an unusual interest in keeping us from finding out the identity of a certain someone." He glanced around the restaurant again and then lowered his voice some more. "I was out in my garage and I found some records that got shoved back in a corner and didn't get taken to the storage room. So the fire didn't destroy them. Just so happens that something you were asking about suddenly became available."

Bobby stood up and motioned to Jenny. "We need to see Elbert right away." He handed Jenny some money. "Take care of the tab and call Elbert. I'll go with Doc."

Doctor Garner nodded. "Have him bring any x-rays he took of the corpse. Meet us at my house. I still have some equipment there to look at the pictures."

~

When Elbert and Jenny arrived, the Doctor had a computer with a large screen set up on a folding table. Bobby, Elbert, and Jenny stared at the images in front of them. On one side of the screen were the x-rays taken of the girl in the box. On the other were those of Emma Johnson from her visits to Doctor Garner. The doctor pointed at the image of Emma's teeth.

"These x-rays of Emma Johnson show a dental reconstruction and oral rehabilitation. What we have is an initial panoramic radiograph x-ray and two mid-treatment periapical x-rays with pictures. The third row of images shows dental x-rays taken after the endodontist completed root canal treatment on three teeth—tooth numbers six through eight." The doctor looked around. "Okay, I'll translate. Emma had two teeth knocked out—broken off. The dentist did root canal work, put in posts and cores and then fitted caps over those. There are also several fillings in various teeth, usually the mark of a high-sugar diet—breakfast cereal with lots of sugar, candy bars, you know. A typical poor diet for kids. Now, if you look at the images that Detective Wainwright brought, you will see the same work. There are the fillings in five, eleven, sixteen and others. And there are the root canals and caps on seven through nine. I know how those teeth were broken and who repaired them because I did the repair work. I also put all those fillings in. I can tell you with one hundred percent certainty that these are matching x-rays. The girl in the box, therefore, is Emma Johnson. She broke those teeth when her drunken step-father struck her brutally in the mouth. Her mother brought her to my office at four o'clock in the morning. It took me eight hours to repair her teeth."

Jenny looked at Bobby. "It's Emma. I just knew it."

∼

ELBERT KNOCKED AGAIN. Finally, the door opened. Chantrice stood there in a rumpled housedress with a sour look on her face. "Again? Don't you people have something better to do?"

Elbert waited for her to quiet. "It's about Emma, Mrs. Edwards."

"Emma! Emma! Well, did you find her in San Francisco like I said?"

Jenny stepped forward. "Closer than that, Chantrice."

"What do you mean?"

"The girl in the box is Emma."

"Now how in the world could you possibly..." Chantrice stopped.

"Doctor Garner compared his dental records with the x-rays of the corpse. A perfect match."

"But I heard..."

"Heard what, Chantrice?"

"Well,... it was all around the village that Dr. Garner's records burned up in the big storage building fire."

Jenny shook her head. "Not all of them, Chantrice. He found some in his garage that he did not move to storage. Emma's records were in there. He told us how you brought her in with her teeth knocked out. Knocked out by Johnny Edwards, your second husband."

Chantrice went white and closed her eyes. "Is it really Emma?"

Elbert nodded. "Without a doubt."

Chantrice looked like she was about to faint. Bobby and Elbert leaped forward and took her under the arms. They helped her inside and walked her to the couch. She sank down with a small moan.

Jenny slipped down beside her. "I'm so sorry, Chantrice. I know this is a shock."

"I always thought she just ran away. Are you sure?" She began to cry. "It can't be my Emma."

Bobby went in the kitchen, found a glass, and poured Chantrice some water. He brought it back and handed it to her. She wiped her eyes with a handkerchief.

She looked up. "Thank you, Sheriff." She took a long drink and sat for a long time. "Emma, Emma, my Emma," she whispered. Then she set the glass down, sighed, and picked up a box that was sitting on the end table. "I found this, Detective. It's a box with some pictures in it. It was in the crawl space above Emma's room. She must have put it there before she left. I was looking up in the attic and found it."

They set the box on the coffee table, opened it, and looked through the items. There were several ribbons, blue and red, on the top. Chantrice held them up. "Emma was a competent artist, amateurish, of course. She used to enter her drawings in the local fair. She won a few ribbons, nothing major, but one day she just tore all the pictures up and never drew again."

The next item was a yearbook from the local high school. Jenny looked inside the front cover, where most annuals had a few blank pages for friends to write comments on. Emma's book only had three comments—one from Dennis and one from someone named Sheryl. The third was from another girl named Pam.

The one from Dennis was a casual note.

"Hey, Emma! Great year, lotsa fun, see you around! Dennis."

Then the one from Sheryl.

"Hey, Emma. Fun hanging out, best of luck in the future. Hope your love life improves. Ha Ha!"

Jenny read it again. *That's odd.*

The one from Pam was just, "*Good Luck!*"

Chantrice pointed to the one from Sheryl. "That's Sheryl Krantz. She liked Dennis, too, so she and Emma had kind of a competition going. He would come pick Emma up from time to time, but I don't think Sheryl liked it when Dennis spent time with Emma alone. The three of them used to hang out... a lot. Here are some pictures of them together."

She picked up some photos and handed them to Jenny. Jenny looked at each one and then passed them to Elbert and Bobby. The first one was in a park. The three kids were sitting at a picnic table drinking what looked like sodas. Dennis was skinny, no shirt, longish, dirty blonde hair and a miserable attempt at a mustache. Sheryl was a good-looking brunette, with a nice figure dressed in a flowered top and Capri pants.

But it was Emma that drew Jenny's eyes. She was a striking girl, not beautiful, but unique in her looks. Her hair was short, almost bobbed, and it was golden. Not yellow, or blonde, but shiny gold. Her eyes were piercing blue and looked right out of the picture. Her face was not what you would call pretty, but it was unusual—thin face, nose straight but a little too big, thin lips compressed in a straight line, almost hard, and a strong, determined chin. The kind of face that would make you look twice.

Chantrice nervously tugged at a bracelet she was wearing and then took the pictures back from Bobby. She looked down at Emma. "Dennis and Emma disappeared at the same time. I always thought they ran away together to San Francisco, and she just forgot about me. Cut me out of her life."

The statement caught Jenny's attention. "Why would she do that, Chantrice?"

"Emma hated me."

"Why?"

Chantrice looked around and Jenny thought she looked like an animal in a trap.

"Because... because..."

"Why, Chantrice?"

"She hated me because I wouldn't protect her."

Jenny took Chantrice's hand. "Protect her from what?"

Chantrice took a deep breath. "From her stepfather."

14
THE TRUTH ABOUT EMMA

Chantrice put her face in her hands. The words came quietly. "I think Emma's stepfather was molesting her... you know... physically. I was sure Emma was sleeping with someone because I found, you know, protection in her drawer. I confronted her. She pretended ignorance, but I knew—mothers know. I asked her if it was Johnny. Johnny was an alcoholic, and he had cheated on me before. She looked at me and laughed and said, 'What if it is?' I told her she was a wicked girl for suggesting such a thing. She said she wasn't doing anything with anybody. So, I asked why she had those things in her drawer. She got very angry and shouted at me. 'In case I find someone to do it with!'"

Jenny put her hand on Chantrice's arm. "Then what happened?"

"I asked Johnny if he was doing anything with her. He was furious. He went to her. He called her a... a whore... and said he would never even think of sleeping with her. And then he said he knew who her lover probably was, said he'd heard gossip. Emma got a look on her face that terrified me. There was a butcher knife on the kitchen counter and she snatched it up and tried to stab him. He hit her, knocked her down. But I was still sure it was him. I never found out because he left me shortly after that."

"Was that the night her teeth were broken?"

"Yes. I took her to the Dentist, and he made me tell what happened. He wanted to have Johnny arrested for assault, but I begged him. I told him how it was Emma's fault. She went crazy and attacked him with a knife and Johnny was only protecting himself. Doctor Garner finally relented. He fixed Emma up good. But she never spoke to me again, and then, a week later, she and Dennis were gone. I thought that was why she never contacted me. Because I didn't listen to her, talk to her, help her. Maybe Johnny wasn't doing anything, maybe she really did have a boyfriend... Oh, it's all so confusing."

Bobby spoke up. "Well, we know this. Your daughter never left town, Mrs. Edwards. Based on the date of Doctor Garner's records and the coroner's estimation, Emma died sometime shortly after her visit to the dentist, within a day or two. So, now we know it's Emma, and we can start looking at suspects."

Elbert picked up the photo with the three kids. "Tell me more about Dennis Cummings."

Chantrice sniffed. "Dennis Cummings was a jerk. He was one of those players, a wise guy. Thought he was a lady's man, always had a smart comeback, always kinda coming on. He even tried it on me, but I gave him what for and he backed off."

Elbert was taking notes. "Did he have a job anywhere? And what about his parents?"

"He was a foster kid. His parents were not around and he bounced from place to place. Dennis couldn't hold a steady job, so he worked odd jobs around town, you know, sweeping out the pool hall or doing yard work for people, but mostly he hung out down at the park, or at the Pizza Hut in the village. He had an old blue Volkswagen bug, and he thought he was great shakes with a guitar. He played around in some of the local coffeehouses and he was always bragging about how he was going to San Francisco to get famous."

Jenny took the picture from Elbert. "Was Emma in love with Dennis?"

"Who knows? She stopped telling me anything a little while after Johnny moved in. She was moody, always listening to records, you know, Pat Boone and The Platters. Just teenager stuff, you know. She withdrew, stayed in her room. She was quiet. I thought it was her hormones. When I found those things in her drawer, her behavior made a little sense, but there was more to it. I couldn't put my finger on it. I thought it was Dennis, but when I think back... I'm not sure. Maybe Dennis, maybe Johnny, maybe someone else. I just don't know. Then when she left and never contacted me, I just figured she'd gone off with Dennis and when I never heard from her again, I knew it was because she hated me."

"Do you have any idea who would want to kill Emma?"

Jenny was watching Chantrice's face and before Chantrice answered, Jenny thought she saw Chantrice's lips pull back for a split second, almost like a snarl.

That was odd...

"Well... Dennis, of course. I heard he was a wild man when he was drunk. I think he had a couple of arrests for assault and battery..." She glanced at Elbert. "... if I'm not mistaken, Detective."

Elbert shrugged. "I'll have to look it up, Mrs. Edwards. That was a long time before I came on the force."

"Well, if you ask me, and I guess you are asking, I think Emma said or did something that riled Dennis up and he was drunk and he hit her and killed her. Then he got out of town and went out to California, like he said he would. It was pretty wild out there back then and he could have just disappeared into the crowds of hippies running around in San Francisco or Los Angeles."

"What's the story with Sheryl Krantz?" Bobby asked. "You said there was some kind of competition between her and Emma for Dennis's affections?"

"Emma told me once that Sheryl really had the hots for Dennis. She kind of laughed when she said it."

"Is she still around? Sheryl?"

"I have no idea. Back then her name was Sheryl Krantz but it could be anything now and she could be anywhere."

"So if she really liked Dennis and Emma was interfering..."

Chantrice nodded. "There were those times when Dennis came and picked Emma up, so it's possible she resented Emma enough about that to kill her. After all, they all drank and did drugs... well, at least I know Dennis did, so anything could have happened if they were high or drunk. And you know kids. They get themselves into some strange situations. I guess I'd put my money on Dennis or Sheryl."

~

Elbert Wainwright sat looking through the files spread out on his desk. Finally, he picked up his phone and punched the intercom button.

"Yes, Detective?"

"Janice, did you find any vehicle registrations for Dennis Cummings?"

"Actually, I did, Detective. I was just about to bring it in."

The door between his office and the reception area opened, and Janice came in with a folder.

"I could only find one record, Elbert. Registered to Dennis Cummings in 1963. A 1958 Volkswagen Beetle. It seems it was his first car. He was 16 at the time and he had to get permission from the state to buy it, since he was in foster care. Cost him $100."

"Any violations or marks against his record?"

"There were. He got two speeding tickets in the first six

months after he bought it. It says he was also in a fender bender, but it turned out to be the other person's fault. He renewed the registration for the first four years he had it, but after 1967, there was no record of it being re-registered. At least not in Ohio."

"Thanks, Janice."

Elbert put the folder on his desk and then looked down at Dennis Cummings's arrest record. Assault and battery, petit theft, drunk and disorderly, minor in possession of marijuana. It was quite a list, but most of it had happened before he was eighteen, so the authorities had been lenient.

He must have wised up after he turned eighteen because there were no more arrests.

Elbert looked at the assault record.

Three cases of misdemeanor assault. First, he threatened to beat up a girl and shoved her around; second one, he grabs a girl and tries to kiss her and she calls a cop; third one, he gets in a fight at the foster home he was living in, threatens the wife with a knife and punches the husband. Sounds like a volatile guy. Wouldn't take much for him to go off on Emma. This has to be our guy.

Elbert put down the papers and went back to the intercom.

"Yes, Detective?"

"Janice, I want you to put the VIN number of Dennis's car into the system and see what you can come up with. Also, can you get me Aaron Sanders on the line? He's out in Sacramento with the Highway Patrol office."

"Did you forget, Detective? In 1958, they didn't have VIN numbers, just serial numbers."

"Put that in and get Aaron on the line."

In a few minutes, Elbert was speaking with his old friend, Aaron Sanders.

"Elbert! Good to hear your voice. What's going on out there in farm country?"

"Not much, Aaron. Been quiet around here since you left for

greener pastures. Livin' the dream out there? Hollywood stars, Mansions at Malibu? Girls in bikinis?"

Aaron laughed. "Man, you were always a flop at geography, Elbert. I'm in Sacramento, not L.A. It's a hick town as far as the upper crust is concerned. The only thing that goes on here is politics and I'm telling you, it's getting crazy out here. Talk about a loony bin."

"Well, at least you're staying out of trouble."

"Yeah, but the longer I live here, the better Wayne County looks to me. So, what can I do for you?"

Elbert pulled the vehicle record out of the folder. "I'm looking for a character named Dennis Cummings. He's a person of interest in a cold case we got going here."

"How cold?"

Elbert chuckled. "Forty years."

Aaron whistled. "That's not a cold case, that's an iceberg. So, what's the skinny?"

"Have you heard about the girl in the box?"

"No, what's that about?"

"We found a girl in a handmade box over in Jepson's woods. Pretty sure she was murdered, skull crushed by a blunt object, jammed into the box, and buried. Turns out she was the daughter of a local woman connected with the Amish community. The mother hadn't seen her since the sixties, thought she ran away to California with a local hippie type, the guy I'm looking for."

"And the mother wasn't curious why her daughter didn't contact her for forty years?"

Elbert tapped his pencil on the desk. "There may have been sexual molestation going on in the home. The step father denied it, so the mother took his side. When the girl disappeared, the mother thought the daughter wanted nothing more to do with her. It's all a little vague."

"So, how can I help you out here?"

"Well, the boyfriend disappeared at the same time and now

he's a person of interest in the case. He told his friends he was west coast bound to get into a rock band. Fancied himself another Eric Clapton or something. I wanted to know if you have any record of him or his car."

"Sure, I can check for you. What's his name?"

"His name is Dennis Cummings. Born in 1947, Wooster Community Hospital, Wayne County, Ohio. Father, unknown, mother, Geraldine Cummings. The vehicle is a 1958 Volkswagen Beetle, serial number 1617345."

"Do you have a VIN number?"

Elbert chuckled. "Didn't have them in 1958. Just serial numbers."

"Gee, Elbert, can you make this a little more difficult? I'm having a boring day."

They both laughed. "I'm sorry, Aaron, but that's all I have."

Elbert could hear Aaron sigh. "Okay, Pal, I'll run this, but don't expect too much."

Elbert hung up. The intercom buzzed.

"Yeah, Janice."

"Jim Stanger from the Cincinnati Police Department on the line."

Elbert spent the rest of the afternoon on the line with agencies across Ohio. By the end of the day, he had drawn a big blank. Nothing. He called Bobby at the motel.

"Hey, Elbert. Any luck with Dennis Cummings?"

"No. It's like the earth swallowed him and his car up. Frustrating. But I have a couple of sheriffs that have to get back to me, so I haven't given up yet. What about you?"

There was a pause, then Bobby spoke. "I'm not so sure Dennis is our perp, Elbert. Call it 'coply instinct.' There are just too many variables. Whoever killed Emma went to a lot of work to hide the body. And where would Dennis get a handmade chest like that? I need to come down and get pictures of the box. Jenny's checking on the ring. I'm going to check the local antique dealers. If we can find out who made the box, we may find out how the killer got the box in the first place."

Elbert shrugged. "Okay, come on over. I've got the coroner's pictures here. There is a duplicate set you can take. I'll have Janice put together a list of the antique stores and woodworkers in the county. I hope you have better luck than I am."

15

MAYBE... MAYBE NOT

Bobby walked out of Thorogood's Antique Store on Main Street. It was the fifth store he had been to that day. He pulled the list from his pocket.

Stoltzfus Antique Delights. In an alley off Clay.

Bobby walked west on Main until he came to Clay. He turned right and walked up the street. On the second block, he came to the alley. He turned in and looked around.

Stoltzfus Antique Delights!

The rickety sign stuck out from a brick wall with a door and two small windows below it. Bobby went in. A bell rang somewhere in the back. The store was bigger than he thought it would be. All kinds of goods crowded every inch of space—furniture, glassware, silver, pictures in decorative frames. A voice came from somewhere in the back.

"*Einen Augenblick!* Just a moment."

In a few seconds, an old man came through a door in the very back of the big room. He was Amish. His long beard was white, and he wore spectacles. He smiled and his eyes twinkled.

"Ah, you come to visit Stoltzfus! Looking for an antique for your wife?"

Bobby smiled.

If he only knew.

"No, sir. I'm actually looking for some information."

"Information?"

"Yes. Have you heard about the girl in the box?"

The old man's face lost its smile. "*Ja*, a terrible, terrible thing. And to happen in Apple Creek. Like when they found that fellow in the pond in his car."

"You remember that? That was 1950."

"*Ja*, dat vas terrible also."

Bobby stuck out his hand. "My name's Bobby Halverson. I used to be the sheriff in Wayne County. But the man in the pond happened before I was the sheriff, pretty soon after I got back from WWII."

Stoltzfus came forward and squinted at Bobby's face. A broad smile broke over his face.

"*Ja, Ja,* Sheriff Bobby. I remember you. I was just a young man then myself. Thomas. Thomas Stoltzfus."

They shook hands.

"How can I help you, Sheriff?"

Bobby grinned. "It's been a long time since I was sheriff, Thomas." He pulled the stack of pictures from his inside coat pocket. "The box they found the girl in was handmade. Pegs instead of nails, mahogany, very well-crafted. It stayed in the ground all those years and didn't rot. I wonder if you could look at these and tell me if you recognize who might have made it."

Bobby handed the pictures to Stoltzfus. The old man moved his spectacles down to the end of his nose and peered at the pictures.

"*Ja*, handmade." He pointed at one picture, a close-up of the corner of the box. "See, the angle of the cut just a tiny bit offline. No electric saw would do that. That was a handsaw." He kept looking. "The pegs are hand shaped and hammered into the joint with a mallet. And he didn't cut the joint straight across. He left a triangular piece on one side and a matching insert on the other so it locks together. Beautiful work. Then he pounded the peg in to hold the corner."

"You say he?"

"*Ja*, only five woodworkers I know who did such work. It was a long time ago, and they were all men."

"Did they live around here?"

Stoltzfus nodded. "*Ja, ja.* Mostly. Two here in Apple Creek, one in Dalton, one up in Wooster, and one over in Moreland."

Bobby smiled. "You remember pretty well, Thomas."

"Well, they all came to me to sell their work. I made a good living off them. I should remember."

"Are they still around?"

"Two have died, I am thinking, but three are alive—one in Wooster, one in Dalton and one over in Moreland. The others have relatives. I can give you their addresses."

"That would be most helpful."

The old man gestured around the shop. "Are you sure nothing for your wife, Sheriff?"

Bobby laughed. "How about something for a friend?"

~

BOBBY SAT with Jenny in the restaurant. Geraldine came over. "I hope you two don't finish your business too soon. I haven't sold this much cherry pie since the quilting festival."

Bobby looked up. "Well, since we finished dinner, I guess we can't break our perfect record. Pie it is."

"Ice cream, Sheriff?"

"You don't even need to ask."

Jenny took Bobby's hand. "The quilting festival. Funny she should mention that. Mama was going to the festival when she became lost in the big storm. I got lost in the big storm, too. She found me and saved me. Then you and Papa came for us. And you've been part of my family ever since."

"Long time ago, Jenny. Lotta water under the bridge." He shook his head and grinned. "And knowing you has never been smooth sailing."

Jenny giggled. "Yeah, like when Jonathan and I ran away and then the drug gang kidnapped me. And you had to round up most of the men in north Pennsylvania to find me."

"Yeah, Jonathan really got me angry when he put you in danger like that. I was going to beat that boy, but then he turned out to be a nice kid."

Jenny smiled. "Very nice. Wonderful."

Jenny stared past Bobby, thinking about Jonathan. Then she remembered. "You know, Bobby, I keep thinking we are missing something. Like when I met Jonathan, and his hippie van and weird clothes almost made me miss who he really was. Remember the morning Rachel and I were talking about how we are looking at a murder where the assumption is somebody randomly killed this girl and then took the time to bury her in the heart of Jepson's woods in a box they got from... from somewhere, right at the time of the crime. Then they got in their car and drove off. But after we started digging, it seems more likely that this was a person who already had the box, killed the girl and then went to great lengths to make sure nobody ever found Emma."

Bobby nodded. "That's what I said to Elbert. He's big on Dennis Cummings being the perp, but how did Dennis get a handmade Amish box to bury Emma in? If Dennis were the erratic person he seemed to be by his record, then if he killed her, he probably would have left Emma in the woods somewhere in a quickly dug grave, and then beat it out of town."

Jenny looked over. "That's right. But that can't be how it happened because whoever did this went to great lengths to make sure nobody found Emma because..."

"... Because they still live right here in Apple Creek."

∽

RACHEL AND DANIEL KING were enjoying the fall afternoon in the Secrest Arboretum in Wooster. They had taken a leisurely stroll through the grounds and admired the fantastic assortment of expertly displayed and maintained flora and fauna. They watched as the many visitors took pictures and pointed out the assortment of birds that flocked in the trees and shrubs. Finally, they unpacked their lunch and were sitting on a bench eating sandwiches when Rachel reached over and touched Daniel's arm.

"What?"

Rachel gave a slight nod with her head. "Don't look too quickly, Daniel, but isn't that the young man that tried to steal *Grossmütter's* box when we first got to town?"

Daniel took another bite and then casually glanced over in the direction Rachel had indicated. The young man was standing by the path through the gardens, seemingly looking at some roses.

"It sure is," Daniel whispered. "What's he doing here?"

Just then, the young man leaped onto the path and grabbed the purse strap of a woman who was passing by.

"Hey! Hey you!" Daniel shouted as he jumped up and gave chase.

The young man looked around, let go of the bag and raced off into the woods with Daniel in hot pursuit.

"Be careful, Daniel!" Rachel shouted.

She waited for a few moments and then Daniel appeared with a sheepish look on his face.

"Rachel, you have to stop feeding me those big dinners. He was fast, and I ran out of breath. He disappeared into the woods."

"We need to go back to Apple Creek and tell Mama and Uncle Bobby."

Daniel nodded. They gathered up the remains of their lunch and headed for the bus stop.

～

BOBBY AND JENNY were finishing their pie when Geraldine came over. "Jenny, it's Rachel. She's calling on the phone. It's over there at the end of the counter."

Jenny got up and went over to the phone. In a few minutes, she came back and sat down. "Rachel and Daniel were in Wooster and they saw the man who tried to steal Mama's box at the station."

"And probably the same man who stole it from the house."

"Yes, Bobby. He was trying to steal a woman's purse when Daniel stopped him."

Bobby took the last bite of pie. "This confirms what we were thinking."

"How so?"

Bobby took out a Camel and then put it away. "I'm guessing this guy is a secondary character in all this. Obviously, he's a petit thief known around town. He probably runs errands for the real crooks. Somebody hired him to steal the box."

"Why do you say that?"

"He's obviously too young to have been involved in Emma's murder. But he knew what the box looked like when he tried to steal it the first time."

Jenny got excited. "Which means that someone who had seen Mama's box in the past described it to him."

"Exactly. So now we are back to Apple Creek. Dennis Cummings could not have killed Emma because he's not here, but there is someone local who has a deep interest in covering everything up." He stood up.

"Where are you going?"

"I'm going to make the rounds of the Amish woodworkers

Stoltzfus told me about. We have to find the person who made the box."

"Good. I'll go down to the police station and see if Elbert can help me track down Sheryl Krantz. She must know something about the time before Emma disappeared. And I think I'll have Daniel and Rachel come down and see if they can look through some mug shots. I'd like to find out who our mysterious thief is."

～

Elbert sat with Jenny and showed her the file. "Sheryl Krantz, 1115 Main Street, Wooster. Doesn't look like she has anything to hide. She's been living in that house for thirty-five years. It belonged to her parents, and they left it to her. She works as a receptionist at Chestnut Ridge Wholesale. Never had an arrest, no record of any kind. Looks like after Cummings left, she took the straight and narrow path."

Jenny nodded. "That was certainly easy. I think we thought she would be missing, too."

Just then, the intercom buzzed. "Yes, Janice. Okay." Elbert released the button and looked at Jenny. "We have a positive ID on our purse snatcher. Come on."

They got up and walked down to the records office. Rachel and Daniel were sitting with an officer. There were several books of mug shots laid out on the table. Rachel pointed to a picture in one of the books. "This is him, Mama. Do you recognize him?"

Sure enough, it was the man that had tried to steal Jerusha's box at the trains station.

Elbert turned the book around and looked. "Gary Walker. Well, well, my old pal, Gary Walker."

Jenny looked at the picture. A thin, pockmarked face, longish stringy hair, a large nose.

"That's him all right. You must know him, right, Elbert?"

Elbert nodded. "Sure do. Gary is one of our usual suspects.

Petit theft, check fraud, purse snatching, drug busts. One year in the state pen for a first-degree assault. Oh yeah, Gary is very well known in Wayne County." He went to the phone and dialed Janice. "Janice, put out an APB on Gary Walker. Yeah, right away. Theft, attempted purse snatching, breaking and entering, the usual." He put down the phone and turned to the group. "Well, it looks like things are heating up. Jenny, you go see Sheryl. I'll take care of rounding up Gary and keeping after Dennis Cummings, and Bobby will visit the woodworkers. We may find out something after all."

16

JOHAN TROYER

*B*obby Halverson was tired. A trip to Dalton, then a trip to Wooster, and now he was on his way to Moreland. He pulled a Camel out and lit it with his WWII Zippo. The years had tarnished the case and the Marine insignia was almost worn off, but it still felt right in his shirt pocket.

He drove into Moreland and pulled up at a local café, Garry's Hotcake House.

I could use some breakfast for lunch.

He walked into the place and the waitress behind the counter called out. "Hey, hon, sit anywhere you want."

Bobby grabbed a small table by the window. Traffic outside on the street was intermittent, and the town seemed to move at a relaxed pace. The waitress ambled over with her pad. Her name tag read "Dee" in all caps. She was an older woman with a ready smile.

"What'll it be, old-timer?" But the question was more respectful than snarky.

Bobby smiled back. "Still serving breakfast, Dee?"

"All day and all night, hon."

"Ah, a restaurant after my own heart."

The waitress grinned. "Thanks for the compliment. Restaurant is a high-toned term for this place. What'll ya have?"

Bobby pulled out the menu that was stuck between the napkin dispenser and the tall sugar shaker. He scanned the breakfast menu. "How about one of those country breakfasts with a side of blueberry pancakes?"

"A man of discernment, I see." She turned to the window behind the counter where Bobby could see the chef working at the stove. "Country and blue short-stack," she called out. She turned back. "Coffee with that?"

Bobby nodded. "Lots and lots, black, please."

"You got it, hon. Back in a minute." She went to the counter and grabbed up the coffee pot and a big mug. She set the mug down in front of Bobby and poured it full. He glanced up. "Can I ask you a question?"

She grinned. "Long as it's not about my love life."

"I'm looking for a woodworker. Been around a long time. His name is Phillip Miller. Know where I can find him?"

"Sure, Phil comes in all the time. Did you come in on Moreland Road?"

Bobby nodded.

"Well, just go back out the way you came and go about three-quarters of a mile back toward Wooster. Look for a sign on the right-hand side. Miller's Wood Creations. Turn in the lane and go right up to his shop."

"Great, thanks."

Just then, the cook pushed two plates through the window. "Country, short stack!"

The waitress hurried over and hustled Bobby's breakfast back. Hash-browns, fried eggs, bacon, and toast, piled high. The stack of hotcakes was still steaming. Dee set a pitcher of syrup and a bowl of whipped butter down beside the plate. "Eat hearty and enjoy."

Bobby set to work with relish.

A half-hour later, Bobby pushed himself back from the table, walked to the register and paid his bill.

Dee looked up from a stack of tickets. "Well...?"

Bobby held his stomach. "If I ate a breakfast like that every day, you'd have to roll me around with a log pike. Fantastic."

"Well, thanks, hon. Have a great day and come back and see us."

"It will probably take a week for this to wear off, but then I will think about it."

He picked up his change and walked out.

"Johan Troyer."

"Johan Troyer?" Bobby glanced at the list Stoltzfus had given him. A name jumped out.

Johan Troyer. There he is.

Phillip Miller pointed to the closeup shot of the peg with the beveled top. "Yep, Johan Troyer. Only woodworker I know who made those beautiful beveled pegs. See how the bevel stands out just a fraction from the surface of the wood? Wouldn't see it if you weren't looking. It was like a signature on all his pieces."

"Was?"

"Yeah, Johan died about fifteen years ago."

"What did you know about him?"

"Johan? Amish. A totally stand-up guy, straight arrow all the way. Made some of the most beautiful cabinets any of us had seen, including me. I wish I could make cabinets like Johan did."

Phillip leafed through the pictures. "This was part of a two-piece kitchen cabinet. This is the bottom half, should be about four feet tall."

Bobby nodded.

"It was for storing bigger pots and pans. There should have been another piece with two doors and racks. It sat on top. You stacked them in a corner." He looked more closely. "Mahogany. Hard as iron. How long did you say it was in the ground?"

"Forty years."

"Wow. It stayed in the ground all those years and still not very stained. Yep, Johan Troyer all right."

Bobby glanced back at his list. "It says here that Johan has a son. Is he a woodworker?"

"Jacob. Well, he dabbles at it, but he's not half the artisan Johan was. He's in Apple Creek, out on Apple Creek Road. He still has his dad's shop. Mostly he farms, but he makes a piece now and again."

"On Apple Creek Road." Bobby looked. There it was—459 Apple Creek Road. "Okay, you have been very helpful, Mr. Miller. Say hi to Dee at Garry's the next time you're in."

Phillip glanced at his watch. "Hey, you're right. I'm late for lunch. Want to join me?"

Bobby patted his stomach. "Maybe in a week or so. Country breakfast…"

"With a short stack. Didn't think you'd get so much food, did you?"

Bobby shook his head. "No, I did not."

∼

Bobby turned in to the driveway. It was a typical Amish farm—small neat clapboard house, red barn, chickens scratching in the yard. One thing that set it apart was the large shop building with a sign that read "Troyer Fine Furniture." It was off to the side and Bobby pulled up in front. As he sat in the car, a man came out of the shop. He was short, bearded and dressed in overhauls and a flannel shirt. The man walked up to the car.

Bobby rolled down the window. "Jacob Troyer?"

The man nodded. "That's right. Can I help you?"

"I'm the former sheriff, Bobby Halverson, and I'm working with the Wooster police Department on a local cold case."

"Ah, the girl in the box."

"Yes, how did you know?"

"Oh, everybody in Apple Creek knows you came in to help Detective Wainwright and you brought Jenny Hershberger with you—because the police were afraid the Amish wouldn't talk to them."

"Well, that's partially correct. Jenny and I know many of the Amish here and the detective thought we might be better received, if the case affected the Amish Community negatively."

"I wouldn't know about the Amish Community."

"I thought you were Amish."

"Were is the operative word, Sheriff. I left the Amish church long ago because of some grace issues. I've been a Mennonite for a long time. If I was Amish, I'd be beardless because I never got married. So, what can I help you with?"

"Well, I have it on good report that your father built the box they found the body in."

Jacob Troyer frowned. "My father? Who told you that?"

"Phillip Miller."

"And how did he identify it so easily?"

"The raised beveled pegs."

"Ah, the raised pegs, my father's trademark. You know, he never showed me how he made those. He died before he could or..."

"Or?"

Jacob shrugged. "He may have wanted to keep the secret for himself. We never really were very close. But there were some others in the area who tried to copy the style. Maybe one of them made the box."

Bobby looked up. "I have some pictures. Maybe you can identify the box. Can I get out of the car?"

"Oh... uh, sure, Sheriff, sorry. Come in, please."

Bobby walked into the shop behind Jacob. It was a large room with benches and racks of hand tools hanging on the wall. Planes, mallets, adzes, handsaws, drills—all the items Bobby would expect to find in a wood-working shop. Bobby reached into his pocket and brought out the envelope with the pictures of the box. He handed it to Jacob. Jacob took them out and began looking at them. He went through the pile once and then again. Finally, he looked up.

"This could be a box my father made. The bevels are the giveaway, of course, but like I said, there were other woodworkers who copied that little detail. It is possible that this is a Troyer cabinet, but I'm not sure."

"Can you look through your father's records and see if you can find any record of it?"

"*Ja,* I can check. It will take me a while because my father was not orderly with his records. And that was forty years ago."

Bobby nodded and filed away the remark.

∼

ELBERT WAINWRIGHT WATCHED as the EMS guys wheeled the gurney into the run-down apartment building. The flashing red and blue lights from the emergency vehicle splashed strange patterns on the weathered lap siding. It was four in the morning and Elbert was not happy about being called out this early. His sergeant came out of the door and beckoned to him. "I want you to tear this apartment inside out. This guy looks like he's been stealing stuff for years."

Elbert watched the guys jack the gurney up the front steps. "So, it's Gary Walker, for certain?"

"That's what the ID says. Kid had a stash in the back room—cameras, laptops, purses, all kinds of stuff. I want it catalogued and checked against the stolen and missing stuff reports."

"Who found him?"

"The landlady. She heard a noise that awakened her, and when she came out into the hall to investigate, Walker's door was partway open and she could see him lying on the couch. She called us right away."

"Didn't go in?"

"Nah, she told us she knew a dead guy when she seen one." He grinned. "Her words."

"Did you find a large sewing box in with the other items?"

"I wouldn't recognize one if I saw it. You'll have to check. And why the interest in Gary Walker?"

"Walker was a person of interest in the Emma Johnson murder."

"The perp?"

Elbert shook his head. "No, he wasn't even born when Emma was killed. But... he's been involved in some interesting incidents connected to the murder—a stolen sewing box, a break-in, maybe a threatening phone call. How did he die?"

"Looks like an overdose, probably meth or heroin. Needle still in the arm. Get to it."

"Sure, Sarge, I'm on it." Elbert walked up the stairs and into the apartment. Matt, the coroner, was finishing up with the body.

Gary Walker. I've been watching this kid go bad since he was eleven years old. Too bad nobody tried to help him.

"What's the story, Matt?"

"Well, from all appearances, it looks like a heroin overdose, but I'm not sure. Look at his face and neck." Matt pulled back the sheet. Gary Walker's face had an open, sardonic grin and his head was arched back in what looked like a spasm. "With heroin, the pupils become tiny, the body is relaxed, in fact the cause of death is the body just forgets to breathe. But here, there's something weird going on, almost like strychnine or something. I've got the hypodermic and I'm going to run tests. I'll let you know in a few hours."

"Thanks, Matt."

Matt turned to the EMS boys. "Okay, he's all yours."

Elbert watched as the body rolled out on the gurney.

"This is really strange, Matt."

"Why's that, Elbert?"

Elbert took his notepad out and reread his notes on Gary Walker. "Just yesterday afternoon, Jenny's daughter picked Gary out of a photo book and made a positive ID as the guy who tried to rob them at the train station. They also saw him try to steal a purse at the Arboretum. I just started looking for him ten hours ago and now he turns up dead. And the other thing... I knew Gary to do a lot of stuff, pop a few pills, smoke a joint, but I didn't know he had moved up to heroin. It's interesting."

"Well. It would make sense, Elbert. The stuff in his bedroom could support a big habit."

Elbert scratched his head. "Maybe. I haven't seen him for a while and he could have gotten strung out. He ran with a dangerous crowd. Still... it's strange." He turned to Matt. "I want to know what was in that shot as soon as you find out."

"Got it—will do. Give me four hours." Matt snapped his bag shut and headed out the door.

Elbert walked into the back room, then stopped and stared. The place looked like a Neiman Marcus catalog. Fancy clothes on racks, laptop computers, pistols, DVD players, purses... a regular Sinbad's cave.

Elbert shook his head and then spoke to the officers who were cataloging the stuff and putting it into boxes. "Don't miss anything, boys. I want to see where all this stuff came from."

He turned and walked down the hall. "Gary, Gary, Gary..."

17
PICTURES

115 Main Street, Apple Creek. I remember walking by this house on the way to the library.

Jenny looked up at the smallish two-story cottage. A wide porch ran across the front and brick pillars held white wooden columns that supported the upper story. A concrete walk led up to the wooden front steps and then meandered around the side of the house. The grass was green and neatly mowed and the flower bed along the front of the porch was free of weeds and waiting for spring planting.

As Jenny stood there, a woman came out with a watering can in her hand. She watered some potted plants on the porch, and then she noticed Jenny standing on the sidewalk. She put down the can and came to the top of the steps.

"Can I help you?"

"Sheryl. Sheryl Krantz?"

"Yes, do I know you?"

Jenny shook her head. An errant silver curl fought its way out from the edge of her *kappe* and tickled against her cheek. "No, I don't think so. I'm Jenny Hershberger. I'm helping Detective Wainwright with an investigation."

Sheryl laughed. "An Amish woman, helping with a police investigation? That's a bit odd. Did someone steal a wheel off the bishop's buggy?"

"I'm afraid it's a bit more serious than that. It's concerning the murder of Emma Johnson."

Sheryl's face went white, and she sat down suddenly on the top step. "Emma Johnson? Murdered? But she ran away with Dennis."

Jenny shook her head. "She never left Apple Creek. You've heard about the girl in the box?"

"Yes."

"That was Emma."

"That was Emma? Murdered? But how, why? And how are you involved?"

"I kind of got dragged into it. May I come up and explain?"

Sheryl rose slowly and beckoned Jenny to come. "Of course. I'm sorry for being inhospitable. Emma Johnson—after all these years. Come sit and tell me."

They sat on a wide couch in the shade. The afternoon sun was bright, but there was a touch of fall in the air. Sheryl excused herself for a minute and came back with a pitcher of lemonade and two glasses. She poured and then sat beside Jenny and looked at her face. "It seems like I should know you."

Jenny took a sip. "I grew up in Apple Creek. My parents were Reuben and Jerusha Springer."

Sheryl's eyes opened in recognition. "Of course, Jenny Springer. You used to work at the library here in Wooster. I spent a lot of time there. I didn't ever say hello because... well, I had heard bad things about the Amish from..."

"Go on."

"Well, I hung out with Emma a lot back then. Her mother had nothing good to say about the Amish. Except..." she paused, "... there was one lady who made a quilt for Emma and that was the only Amish person Mrs. Edwards ever said anything good about."

Jenny smiled. "Yes, that was my mother. Whoever killed Emma wrapped her in that quilt before they buried her. That's why Detective Wainwright invited me to help with this case. He called me in because the case seemed to point to the Amish community and I used to be the historical intern at the library. I know most of the history of Apple Creek and all the Amish in it, so he thought I might be a liaison for his office, someone who the Amish would trust if things got dicey. It got complicated, though, when I recognized the quilt as one my mother made. That's how we found Chantrice, Mrs. Edwards."

"How's that?"

"My mama made several what she called her blessing quilts. She made them as gifts for people who just needed to know that somebody cared. Chantrice had a tough time when she was young and..."

"Yeah, the Amish threw her out."

"Yes, they shunned her because she got pregnant. So, my mama made her a quilt."

"And it became Emma's security blanket." Sheryl looked down at her hands. "Emma never knew her grandparents. But she always wanted to know about the Amish. It used to make her mother furious. So Emma stopped asking. But she still wanted to know. The quilt your mom made was like a contact for her, a touchstone to her past."

Jenny smiled. "Yes. I have a quilt just like that. My mama made that one, too." Jenny put down her lemonade. "You said Emma ran away with Dennis. So, Emma really was Dennis's girl friend?"

Sheryl shook her head. "No, she wasn't. Emma and Dennis were never an item."

Jenny stared at Sheryl. "But Chantrice said..."

"Mrs. Edwards just said that because they both disappeared at the same time and that's how she explained Emma leaving.

Emma hated her mother, and Mrs. Edwards knew it. So, it was a good excuse. I think she suspected..."

"... that her husband was molesting Emma?"

Sheryl got a very surprised look on her face. "I never heard about Johnny Edwards molesting Emma, although he was a creep and it could have happened. No, Emma... Emma..."

"What about Emma, Sheryl?"

"Emma was very serious about someone, someone in the area. She was very much in love with him. But she swore me to secrecy, and she never told me who it was. Chantrice Edwards might have made that story up after she beat Emma and broke her teeth."

"Chantrice beat her?"

"That's what Emma told me."

"But why? Chantrice told me Johnny hit her."

"Her mom found out about what Emma was doing, that she was, you know, sleeping with someone. She beat Emma good, broke her teeth. When Mrs. Edwards took her to the dentist, she told the doctor Emma flew into a rage about something Johnny said and tried to kill him, and he hit her in self-defense. But Emma told me the truth."

"So, Johnny Edwards wasn't molesting Emma?"

"Maybe, but not that I knew of. If he was, Emma never told me. I think she would have because we were very close. Emma's mother was the weird one. She never got over her mother and father throwing her out and banning her from the Amish."

"So where is Johnny Edwards now?"

"Johnny Edwards left Chantrice a few months after Emma disappeared. He just took off."

"Do you know where he went?"

Sheryl thought for a moment. "I think he went back east. He was from Maine or someplace like that."

"So, all these years, you thought Emma ran away with Dennis?"

"What else could I think? When they both disappeared..."

"How do you know Dennis and Emma weren't involved?"

"Dennis and Emma weren't an item because Dennis was in love with me."

"What?"

"When Dennis and Emma disappeared, I just couldn't understand what happened. Dennis and I had been talking about going to San Francisco for months. We were madly in love. I loved him and I know he loved me. And besides, Emma was in love with her mystery man."

"What happened before Dennis left?"

Sheryl sighed. "He came to my house one night and said he had the money to go to California. He told me he was going to go over to get it and he'd only be gone a few hours. I was supposed to pack my things, and he'd come for me. He never came back. I waited all night and all the next day. Then when I went to Emma's house, she was gone, too. Her mother hadn't seen her. When I didn't hear from either of them for a week, I just thought they had gone away together. I thought they had betrayed me. I never heard from either again."

Jenny saw tears start from Sheryl's eyes. She put her hand over Sheryl's.

"You really loved him, didn't you?"

Sheryl put her hands to her face and began to sob. She cried for several minutes. Jenny comforted her as best she could. Finally, the paroxysm of grief passed and Sheryl sat up.

Jenny handed her a hanky and Sheryl wiped her eyes with it.

"You never married."

Sheryl shook her head. "Dennis was the only man I ever loved. Oh, I know he had his faults, but to me, he was sweet and gentle. He had a troubled life because his parents abandoned him, but he was getting it together. He acted tough and pretended he was a lady's man, but he was very shy. It was all a bluff to keep people from getting to him. He was an excellent guitarist, and he wrote wonderful songs. He used to sing them for me."

Jenny smiled. "My Jonathan was a singer, too. He wrote some songs that a band recorded and they became very well known. But that was in another life and that's another story."

"That's interesting Jenny. I always wondered why Dennis didn't become famous himself. I kept waiting to hear about the great band he was in with hit records. When I went to the record shop, I always looked at the latest hit records, trying to find something he had done. He was so good. But I never saw him or heard about him." She took a deep breath. "And now, after all these years, you come to tell me that Emma never left Apple Creek, that she was murdered. Where's Dennis then? Why didn't he take me with him? Oh, I thought all this was over. Now it's all back again."

Jenny nodded. "I know. It's difficult, but I think we are getting close to finding the answer. Do you have anything that would help in the investigation? Pictures, or notes?"

"Sure, I have a box of stuff. Let me get it."

She got up, and then as she went in the door, she turned. "It will be easier to look at the things at the dining room table. Come on in."

Jenny got up and went into the house. It was very neat and tidy, with beautiful landscapes on the walls and very stylish furniture, antique-y, and well taken care of. Sheryl came out of a side room with a cardboard box and motioned toward the dining room.

"Your house is delightful, Sheryl. Somehow it's not what I..."

"Expected from an old druggie?" Sheryl laughed. "Well, If I had inherited it back in the day, I probably would have sold it and spent the money. Fortunately, I got my life turned around before my parents died."

"What happened? Did you go to AA or something?"

"No, I gave my life to Christ. Very simple. One day I was lost, and the next I was found. The best day of my life."

"That's wonderful. I'm a Christian, too."

"Well, you would expect that, you being Amish and all."

Jenny sat down at the table. "Unfortunately, that's an assumption that doesn't fit the actuality."

"How so, Jenny?"

"Many Amish have a cultural Christianity, but they do not have a genuine relationship with Jesus. They think that keeping the *Ordnung* will give them right standing with God. Somewhat like Orthodox Jews trying to keep the Law of Moses. Many do not understand that the law cannot save you..."

"... because only Jesus can do that, right?" Sheryl smiled and put the box down. "So, I had my life headed in the right direction and when my folks died, they left me this house. My dad saw the change in me, and he knew I would take care of it. It was a blessing. I've tried to honor them by keeping it as nice as they did." Sheryl reached for a Kleenex in a box on a shelf and dabbed her eyes. "Today seems to be a crying day. But good."

They laughed. "That's a wonderful story, Sheryl. I don't know what I'd do without Him either."

"Well, let's look at this stuff. If I cry again, Jenny, just bear with me. I really don't know why I kept it." She pulled out some pictures—the three of them at what looked like the park. Dennis, Sheryl, and there was Emma again, so intense looking with her short-cropped golden hair and angular features—not beautiful in the classic sense, but very striking. Dennis Cummings was a handsome boy, his long hair pulled back in a ponytail.

Just like Jonathan when I first met him. How strange that we both had a very similar experience at the same time in our lives, me Amish, and her Englisch.

Sheryl pulled a rolled-up piece of art paper out of the box. "I have something interesting, something Emma's mother never knew I had." She unrolled it slowly. It was a charcoal drawing, several sketches of the same man. The man was Amish.

"That is interesting. Did Emma draw this?"

"Emma was a brilliant artist. She won prizes at the fair, but her mother always made fun of her. So, she told her mother she tore up all her drawings, but she actually gave them to me to keep for her."

"You have more?"

Sheryl reached down in the box and brought out a sheaf of the rolled-up drawings. Slowly, she unrolled them on the tabletop. They were drawings from Apple Creek, mostly of the Amish. There were men in buggies, women sitting and chatting, men in the fields harvesting. The pictures were beautiful. She pulled out one last picture. It was a full face of the man from the first drawing—actually, a beardless youth, probably about seventeen or eighteen.

"Do you know who this is?"

"No. I just thought she was obsessed with the Amish, so I never asked her. It was a kid who hung around the park. She saw him in the park one day, so she asked him if she could draw him. I think he was on *Rumspringa*. I might have a photo of him. Let me see."

She pulled out another set of pictures and thumbed through them. On the fifth one, she stopped. "Yes, there he is, kind of part way into the picture. A friend of ours took this of all of us."

Jenny looked. There were Dennis and Sheryl, and Emma, sitting on a table in the park. Behind them a young Amish man stood looking at the three of them, a smile on his face.

"So, you don't know him?"

Sheryl wrinkled her brow. "I think he told us his name once, but for the life of me I can't remember."

"Can I borrow this picture, Sheryl? I'll make a copy and bring it back tomorrow. I think Bobby and Elbert will be interested."

Sheryl handed her the picture and Jenny got up. As she

turned to leave, Sheryl asked a question. "Jenny, was Emma wearing a charm bracelet when they... I mean... when the coroner examined her?"

"No. She had a ring, but no bracelet."

"A ring? That's odd. Emma never wore a ring. The only thing she ever wore was that stupid charm bracelet. Different kinds of fish charms. That and the quilt were the only things she really had. Oh, well."

Jenny had a tiny memory come into her head and then fade away.

A charm bracelet. Now where did I see a charm bracelet?

18
A FALL IN THE DITCH

The two hikers made their way through the fantastically overgrown woods of Grosjean Park outside Wooster. They had driven in on a dirt road past the skate park and at the end, they found the little kiosk with the sign. They picked a direction and started walking through the underbrush. Soon they came upon a path leading past various posts with numbers on them.

The girl looked at the posts. "What do you suppose those were?"

The young man shrugged. "Maybe old campsite markers?"

"Did they used to let campers in here?"

The young man pulled out a power bar, unwrapped it, broke it in half and handed a piece to the girl. "I don't know. I never heard of any. I guess I don't know what they are for."

They hiked on, following the path down to a creek. The creek was wide, but shallow, running over stones and then twisting out of sight around a bend ahead. The girl dipped her fingers in the water. "This must be Apple Creek."

The young man nodded. "Probably. If we followed it, we

would end up where it flows into Killbuck Creek, out by Blanchley Road."

The girl pushed through some brush as they made their way along the path. "Why is it so overgrown in here?"

The man shrugged. "They never intended it for hiking. Old Alice Grosjean donated this land in 2001. It was private land before that and back then it was almost wilderness. Mainly, they use the creek as a trout release point, so they try to discourage people from coming in."

They walked on in silence. The fall sunlight fell pale through the overarching branches. A slight chill was in the air and they were glad for their wool over-shirts. A tiny breeze stirred the leaves of the brush and trees.

The day was an Ohio painting, clear blue sky, puffy white clouds, and the scent of fall all around them. The girl stopped and smelled the air. A smoky scent drifted in on the breeze. "I love it when people burn their leaves. And the cornstalks in their gardens."

The young man nodded. "I should have brought my fly rod. I bet there are some lunkers down in the creek."

"We didn't come to go fishing, Pete. This is my day to have you all to myself."

They stopped and stood in the silence. Far away a train, headed west, gave a long blast on the whistle. "Such a lonesome sound," she said. "Do you ever wonder where they are going? Or what their stories are, I mean the men and women who ride the train? I should write about it sometime."

The man nodded. "You're a talented writer, Connie. You should write a book."

"Yeah, me and Hemingway."

"No, I mean it. I've read the articles you write for the paper."

"I never could."

"I think you should think about it and I think I'm going to keep pushing you."

A FALL IN THE DITCH

She flushed and looked at him. "You think I could?"

"Absolutely."

They walked on. He took her hand, and she looked over at him. After a while, they came to an old dirt road that angled upward along a deep gully. They walked uphill for about ten minutes. Then the girl stopped and walked over to the edge of the road. "What do you think that plant is that seems to blanket all the banks? It looks like Japanese Hops. That's a noxious weed." She stepped off the road and reached down to pick some.

"Careful..." the young man warned.

As she stepped down, a rock turned under her foot, and she lost her balance. Suddenly, she was sliding down the side of the gully into a wildly overgrown patch of underbrush. She disappeared from the young man's view. He called out. "Connie! Connie!"

There was silence for a moment and then her voice came back from out of the pile of brush. "Pete, I think I twisted my ankle, but I'm okay. I slid down on my backside so I didn't roll or anything. You'll have to climb down and get me. It's open underneath the brush."

The young man dropped his pack. "On my way, hold tight." He scrambled over the edge of the bank and worked his way down. When he came to the brush, he had to push his way through. He discovered the gully was deeper than he thought. The brush that looked like it was covering the bottom of the gully was really six feet up the sides and overarched all the way across. Below it was an open space. Connie was sitting there, rubbing her ankle.

"I really turned it."

"Can you stand up?"

He took her under the arms and lifted her. She stood in his arms on one leg. He kissed her full on the mouth.

"Pete! You're naughty." She smiled and kissed him back.

"Well, it seemed an opportune moment." He kissed her again.

She turned her head. "Okay, lover boy. Let's stop fooling around and get me out of here."

"Okay, see if you can put your weight on it."

She straightened her leg and gently set her foot down. She stood that way for a moment and then put a little more weight on it. She winced, but then kept going until she was standing on both feet.

"Yeah, I turned it, but I don't think it's sprained. If you help me, I think I can get up the hill."

He turned her around and supported her under her arm. They started slowly up the bank when something caught the girl's eye... something blue.

"Pete, what's that?"

"What's what?"

"There's something blue over there, under that brush. Put me down and go look."

Pete helped her sit down and then he went over to the pile. He could see something through the branches. It was blue, and it was big. He started pulling the brush away. In a minute, he was staring at a car.

An old blue Volkswagen Bug.

∽

Elbert picked up the phone. "Elbert Wainwright. Yes, Trooper Garrity, sure I remember. You found what? An old blue Volkswagen in Grosjean Park? With a body inside?" Elbert sighed. "I'll be right out."

∽

Elbert watched from the top of the bank as the tow truck driver adjusted the cable under the front of the car. A couple of city park workers with chainsaws stood off to the side next to the pile of brush they had cut away from around the car. Behind him, the two hikers sat on the bank on the other side of the road.

Elbert called down. "I hope you boys didn't disturb the site too much."

One of them grinned. "Naw, Detective. We watch Law and Order too, ya know. We were very careful."

The driver climbed back up and got into the truck. He turned on the motor and then climbed out and lowered the support jacks in the back. The young hiker walked up to Elbert. "Do you need us anymore? I need to get Connie home. She twisted her ankle pretty good when she fell and it's swelling a little."

"No, I don't think I need you anymore today. I would like to have you come down to the station and write out a report for me. How far is your car?"

"Just down the trail. We're good."

"Thanks for calling this in."

The young man nodded. "Lucky. I rarely carry my cell phone when I'm hiking, but I threw it in my pack this morning. Will tomorrow be all right to come in?"

"Yeah, perfect. See you then."

The two young people walked off and Elbert turned back to the scene in front of him. The driver manipulated the levers in the console, lifted the tow arm, and extended it over the side of the gully. Then he shifted a lever, tightening the cable. The blue car moved. It turned sideways until it was facing up the bank and then slowly the cable dragged the car upwards. All the tires were flat, so it didn't roll, it scooted. Carefully, the driver wound the cable onto the winch, and the blue car came out of the gully. In a few minutes, it was up on the road and the police gathered around it. Elbert carefully brushed away some dirt from the rolled-up window and looked through. Slumped on the passenger side were skeletal remains. Still clinging to the skull was some long, blonde hair.

"Dennis Cummings! Well, there you are."

The officer next to Elbert looked in. "Who?"

"Dennis Cummings. Been missing for forty years. And the bodies keep piling up. What in the heck is going on here?"

∽

Elbert, Bobby, and Jenny sat around Elbert's desk. Elbert opened the file. "It was Dennis Cummings all right. His Volkswagen, the dental records are a match, got his ID and his stuff in the car. Even the guitar is a match. So, I think we are done here. I think we got our perp, and I want to close this up and go home."

Bobby folded his hands over his stomach and shook his head. "If Dennis is the perp, what's the scenario for this crime, Elbert?"

Elbert picked up a pencil and tapped it on the desk. "I think Emma and Dennis were going to run away. Something happened. Maybe Emma ticked him off and Dennis killed her, probably in a drunken rage. He puts her in the box, buries her in the woods and heads west out of town. He's drunk, so he gets lost and winds up on old lady Grosjean's property. While he's looking for a way out, he drives up the road, runs off the cliff. He crashes through the brush, hits his head on the way down, and kills himself. The car, hidden under the brush, stays down in the gully where nobody goes. Dennis, dead as a doornail, decomposes for forty years until a couple of hikers find him."

"Interesting scenario, but completely full of holes."

"How so, Sheriff?"

"Where did he get the Amish handmade box? If he was drunk, why did he take the time to put her in the box, drag it out to Jepson's Woods and bury her? How did he get the box into his little Volkswagen? Why didn't he just dump her in the woods and beat it? Why is Gary Walker dead? Who made the threatening phone call to Jenny? And the list goes on."

Elbert slumped in his chair. "Yeah, I know. I guess I'm trying to make this as simple as I can so..."

Jenny smiled. "So you can get shut of it?"

Elbert nodded. "Yes, actually. This whole mess is wearing on me. Emma is dead, Gary is dead, and now Dennis is dead. We got three dead people and the soup just keeps getting thicker. And the sheriff and my sergeant are turning up the heat. Not to mention a rumble from the Amish around here."

The phone on Elbert's desk rang. Elbert picked it up. "Wainwright. Oh, hi, Matt, what's up? Two things? Yeah, go ahead, shoot."

Elbert listened to Matt, and he nodded. "Okay, thanks for the info. Yeah, talk to you later."

He put the phone back on the receiver.

Jenny scooted forward in her chair. "What, Elbert?"

"Matt found out two things for me. Number one, the injection that killed Gary Walker was heroin mixed with strychnine—a hot shot, they call it. He died almost immediately. Somebody killed him, and that somebody getting out the back door was probably what woke the landlady up. And second, Dennis Cummings was murdered too. Someone smashed the back of his skull in, just like Emma's. And the blow was not consistent with plunging off the cliff. Someone hit him with a heavy, blunt object, like a hammer from behind. Hit him a lot. So now we are back to square one."

Jenny stared over at Elbert and then looked at Bobby. "And we have a desperate killer who will go to any lengths to keep us from finding them. Someone that is right under our noses."

19
JOHAN'S BOX

The three of them stared at each other. Finally, Elbert spoke. "Sheriff, are you armed?"

Bobby nodded.

"Good. I am also going to put a stakeout on your house, Jenny. It seems we've stirred up a hornet's nest. Somebody who thought this crime was in the past is getting very anxious—anxious enough to kill Gary. And that means that you might be in danger."

Bobby patted the bulge under his arm. "I don't want you to be alone, Jenny. If you go out I'll go with you."

Jenny looked over at Bobby. "Well, killing Gary is one thing, because they tried to make it look like an overdose. But if they tried anything with me, wouldn't that bring way too much attention?"

"True, but I don't think we are dealing with a rational person. This person is desperate, and that means they will do desperate things."

Jenny nodded. "Okay, I'll do what you want. So, what's next?"

Bobby leaned back in his chair. "When I asked Jacob Troyer

about the box, he was vague. Said it could be his father's work, but there were a lot of other guys that were copying Johan's work back then. But I think he was sandbagging me. Now, Phillip Miller told me that the box was part of a two-piece kitchen cabinet. Maybe Stoltzfus can tell me if he ever saw the top half. And if we can find it we can prove without a doubt that Johan Troyer made the box."

"Do you think Johan is the killer?"

Bobby shook his head. "Johan has been dead for a long time. If he did it, why would someone else go to this much trouble? Killing a small-time crook like Gary Walker is foolish if you were not involved in the original crime. I think Gary knew something that would blow this case wide open, something that would expose our perp."

Elbert agreed. "So, what we have is a person who committed the crime forty years ago and thought they had gotten off scot-free, suddenly having to cover their tracks again."

"That's right—which is why we need to protect Jenny." Bobby turned to Jenny. "I think you should get a magnifying glass and go over that ring with a fine-tooth comb. There just might be a jeweler's mark. I'm betting it's locally made and if we can find the jeweler, that would be a great help. Elbert, you need to have forensics go over Dennis's car with the same comb. Maybe the killer left some evidence."

Jenny knit her brow. "So, we narrowed our list down. Who are we looking at now?"

Elbert opened his notebook. "Okay. Gary and Dennis are off the list, which leaves Johan Troyer or Sheryl Krantz."

"What about Johnny Edwards? Sheryl said he went back to Maine. Shouldn't we talk to him?" Bobby asked.

Jenny shook her head. "Our killer is right here in Wayne County, right under our noses. And I don't think it is Johan or Sheryl. In fact, I know it's not Sheryl. It's someone we are getting close to. We just don't know who it is yet."

Jenny sat in the evidence room, examining the ring. She had the bright table lamp directly overhead, and she had a magnifying glass. She looked closely at the ring. There was the inscription, *Ewige Liebe.*

Eternal Love. Someone was crazy about Emma.

A picture came into Jenny's mind—The young Amish man in Emma's drawings. She remembered the detail Emma had put into the face, the eyes. The young man was not a stranger to Emma.

Of course. That young man was not just a random subject. Emma was in love with him and he with her. You could see it in the drawings.

She turned the ring over. Nothing on the outside. She looked at the inside again. Across from the inscription was a tiny discolored spot left by the decaying finger.

Gold doesn't tarnish, so this spot should come off.

Jenny walked over and asked the officer behind the desk if he had a swab and some rubbing alcohol. He went to a drawer and then came back with the requested items. Jenny sat down at the table and gently swabbed the spot. The stain came off. There was something there. She swabbed some more and then there it was. A tiny mark. She looked closer. It was two letters, a "V" and an "A".

VA. I need to ask Elbert.

She put the ring back in the glassine evidence package and handed it to the officer. "I'll need this later," she said, and walked down the hall to Elbert's office. Janice was sitting at her desk. She looked up when Jenny came in.

"Hi Jenny. Elbert is going over the car with forensics. Can I help you?"

"Are there any jewelers in the area with the initials VA?"

Janice pulled out a phone book. "Sit down, we'll take a look." She turned to the yellow pages and ran her finger down the list.

"Here's one. Victor Albert, Master Jeweler. He's right here in Wooster. On East Bowman Street. Here's the address." She jotted down the number and handed it to Jenny.

"Thanks, Janice. Would you mind if I used your phone to call Bobby?"

Janice smiled. "Not at all, Jenny."

~

Bobby walked into Thomas Stoltzfus's shop. The bell in the back rang and Thomas's voice floated out. "Be right out." In a moment, Thomas bustled out. "Oh, Sheriff Halverson."

Bobby reached into his pocket and pulled out the packet of pictures. "Hello, Thomas. Yes, I'm back again."

"How can I help you?"

"I talked to Phillip Miller, and he is positive Johan Troyer made the box. He pointed out the beveled pegs raise just a fraction of an inch about the surface of the box."

"Ja, ja, the beveled pegs. That was Johan, all right. I should have remembered that."

"But when I went to his son, Jacob, he said that other woodworkers were copying Johan's trademark and it could be them who made the box."

Thomas shook his head. "*Nein*, not likely. I have seen no one who could do what Johan did with pegs. Let me look again."

Bobby put the closeup of the pegs on top and handed him the pictures. Thomas scanned them. "*Ja*, Johan Troyer all right. I'm pretty sure. Not sure we could prove it, though."

Bobby took the pictures back. "Well, maybe there is. Phillip Miller said the box was part of a set, a kitchen cabinet in two pieces. The box they buried the girl in was the bottom half. Did you ever see the top half?"

Thomas thought a moment and then the penny dropped. "The top half? Of course, the top half. *MeineMit Gott im Himmel!*

Kumme Mit mir." He led Bobby through the maze of displays and cabinets until they came to a cabinet with two doors that were open, showing racks with pans and utensils hanging in order. "This is the top half of the cabinet. I just remembered. Johan brought this to me a year before he died. He wanted to know if I could sell it without the bottom. He said someone stole the bottom half. It is such a beautiful piece, I bought it for myself. I use it as a display case. I'm sorry I did not recognize it when you first showed me the pictures. But the old box was so stained..."

Bobby dug out the pictures and compared them with the display case. Except for the discolorations on the burial box, the two pieces were obviously from the same set.

Stoltzfus nodded his head vigorously. "*Ja, ja,* Johan Troyer. No one else could make such a cabinet."

"Well, well. Johan Troyer. I'll have to pay a visit to his son."

Just then, Bobby's cell phone rang. He pulled it out and answered. "Halverson. Yeah, Jenny. Albert Victor in Wooster? Sure, stay there and I'll come pick you up."

Bobby put his phone back and grabbed Thomas's hand. "Thanks so much, Thomas. You've been a great help."

"Well, I hope you find this killer. Then the Amish around here can get back to their lives."

∼

VICTOR ALBERT LOOKED at the ring under his loupe. He looked up and nodded. "Yes, I made this ring a long time ago. That's my mark." He held the ring up to the light. "I remember this ring. I made it for an Amish lad. Said he was going to ask his girl to marry him, but he didn't know if she would accept. He wanted it plain gold with the inscription. He paid me cash for it."

Jenny took the ring back. "Do you have the name of this young man?"

Victor took his glasses off and thought for a moment.

"Hmmm, Gerald, no... Jonathan, no... Well, let me look in my book."

He went behind his counter and looked at a rack with several accounting books lined up in it. "Let's see, 1961, 1962, 1965, here it is. 1967. Let's look." He pulled out the book and thumbed through it. "Let's see... Gold rings, gold rings, gold... okay. Yes, this is the one. A small gold ring with the inscription *Ewige Liebe* in German. Sold to... let me see."

Jenny leaned over the counter. Victor looked up. "Sold to Jacob Troyer."

~

ELBERT STOOD PATIENTLY, watching his forensics man's legs wiggle around as they stuck out of the car. "Lots of dust in here, Detective. Looks like it drifted in through the cracks in the window. Very fine." He sneezed and a small cloud of dust puffed out the door. He wriggled some more and then turned partway on to his side. "Hey! Found something, detective. It was wedged up under the front seat. Could be the murder weapon." He backed out of the car and stood up. Dust mixed with perspiration streaked his face. Elbert pulled on a pair of vinyl gloves as the forensics officer handed him what looked like a pestle. Elbert took it by the very end. The object was solid wood. It was one piece with a thick rounded end that tapered down to a handle that ended in a knob. It was heavy. The officer pointed to the thick end. "Definitely something that could do damage if you struck someone with it."

Elbert looked at the officer.

"Do you know what it is?"

The officer brushed himself off. "Yeah. It's a carver's mallet. Something a woodworker would use when he was carving and shaping with a knife and he needed to tap the back of the blade. Or you would use it with a mortise chisel. It's hardwood of some sort, probably beech."

"Do you think we could get fingerprints?"

"Maybe. We'll look carefully. Fingerprints can last up to forty, forty-five years depending on the environment they are in. There's also what looks like some hair and skin stuck to the surface of the front."

Elbert carefully rotated the mallet. Something was carved on the back. He handed it to the forensics guy. "Brush this out carefully. Don't disturb the hairs or any prints."

The forensics officer picked up a tiny brush and cleared out the marks carved into the wood.

"Initials, Detective, most likely the owner. And they say J.T."

∽

SHERYL KRANTZ HAD Emma's drawings spread out on the dining room table. Emma had been a brilliant artist. The buggies, the landscapes of the farms, the Amish men harvesting, Amish women in the market. She had captured them perfectly. She came to the drawings of the young man. Emma had really outdone herself with these sketches. She had captured everything about him, the slight smile on his lips, the angles of his face, the love in his eyes...

Sheryl looked again. Yes, she was right. There was love in those eyes, deep love.

It's him! Emma's lover.

She got up and began pacing.

What was his name? He told me his name when we were hanging out that day. What was his name?

Then it came to her. She went to the phone and called the number at the police station Jenny had given her.

"Elbert Wainwright."

"Detective Wainwright? This is Sheryl Krantz. Is Jenny there?"

"No, she's checking on some things. How can I help you?"

"Can you tell her I just remembered the name of the Amish

kid that was hanging around Emma? I'm sure he was the one Emma was in love with."

"What's the name?"

"Jacob Troyer."

20

JACOB

The police cars rolled onto the Troyer farm about five o'clock in the afternoon. Elbert climbed out of his cruiser and signaled for his men to surround the building. Bobby and Jenny were in the back of Elbert's car. Elbert leaned in the window. "Stay behind me."

They got out of the car and Elbert motioned for his men to go in. They did, guns drawn.

In a minute, they called. "All clear, Detective."

Elbert, Jenny, and Bobby went into the shop. Jacob Troyer was sitting at his desk with his face in his hands. He looked up at Jenny. "*Also ist es endlich vorbei.*"

Jenny saw his face full in the light.

It's him, the boy from the drawings! He's older, he has a beard now, but it's him!

Elbert pulled out the glassine envelope and put the ring on the desk in front of Jacob.

"Do you recognize this?"

Jacob picked it up and looked at the inscription inside. He nodded. "*Ja,* that is the ring I gave Emma."

Elbert put the mallet in front of Jacob. "And this?"

Jacob nodded. "My father's mallet. But where...?"

"We found the mallet in Dennis Cumming's car. The ring was on Emma's finger."

"I do not know how the mallet got in Dennis's car."

"But you admit you gave this ring to Emma?"

"*Ja, ja.* I gave it to her."

"Jacob Troyer, I am arresting you for the murder of Emma Johnson."

Jacob said nothing, just nodded.

Elbert continued. "And the murder of Dennis Cummings and Gary Walker."

A surprised look came over Jacob's face. "Dennis Cummings? Dennis is dead? But I didn't kill him. And who is Gary Walker?"

Elbert continued. "You have the right to remain silent. Anything you say can be used against you in court. You have the right to talk to a lawyer for advice before we ask you any questions. You have the right to have a lawyer with you during questioning. If you cannot afford a lawyer, one will be appointed for you before any questioning if you wish. If you decide to answer questions now without a lawyer present, you have the right to stop answering at any time."

Jacob had a confused look on his face. "*Ja*, it doesn't matter now. You know I killed Emma or you wouldn't be here. I didn't mean to, I didn't mean to. But I didn't kill Dennis, I didn't kill him."

Elbert nodded to his men. "We'll talk about all that down at the station. Is this where it happened?"

Jacob looked around. "Yes, it was here."

Jenny glanced around. She was standing by a large work table. Something didn't feel quite right about all of this. Especially the obvious surprise on Jacob's face when Elbert told him about Dennis and Gary. The room was large and there were tools hanging on the walls, several benches and work tables around the room. Jenny felt something in her spirit.

Gott, show me the truth. Help me with this.

The sun was low on the horizon and as it moved toward sunset, a bright ray came through the sparse clouds and in the window. Out of the corner of her eye, Jenny saw a tiny sparkle of light for an instant in a crack under the table. She bent down. Something was in the crack—buried under years of sawdust and trimmings. Just the smallest part was exposed, and that part had sparkled for just an instant. Jenny reached down, pushed away the debris, and dug it out of the crack.

A fish charm? Sheryl said Emma always had a fish charm bracelet. Where did I see a charm bracelet with fish like this?

She slipped the charm into her pocket. And then she remembered.

∽

JACOB TROYER SAT in an interrogation room at the Wooster police station. He was pale but collected. Elbert sat across the table. Another officer sat on a chair in the corner of the room. In a room adjacent, Bobby and Jenny watched on a tv screen.

Elbert looked over at Jacob. "Do you want an attorney present?"

Jacob shook his head. "It doesn't matter. I have lived with this so long I just want to get it off my chest."

"Tell me what happened, Jacob."

Jacob looked down at his hands. "First, I want to tell you, I don't remember killing her."

"What do you mean?"

"I mean, I was drunk and fell down and I must have blacked out and when I woke up, Emma was dead."

"Okay, let's hear the story from the beginning."

"I met Emma when I was on *Rumspringa*..."

∽

EMMA JOHNSON and Sheryl Krantz climbed out of Dennis's car. It was a late August evening in 1967. It was still hot out and the girls had dressed in shorts and halter tops. They were all going to the park. Dennis leaned out the window. "You guys stay here. I'm going to see if I can get some stuff. My guy said he was going to get something superb. I'll be back in a while."

Sheryl smirked. "Yeah, right? You go over to your friend's house and, of course, you have to try it out and then four hours from now you might show up and you might not."

Dennis grinned. "You got me pegged, girl. But what if the dude tries to slip me oregano or something? Gotta make sure before I shell out my hard-earned coin."

"Dennis, you are incorrigible. Go ahead. See you later."

"Wait," Emma said. She leaned into the back of the car and pulled out her quilt. She saw Sheryl's look and shrugged. "We need something to sit on. I don't want to get my legs all itchy in the grass."

The girls walked to a large sycamore tree. Sheryl carried Emma's sketch pads and pencils.

"Thanks for keeping my drawing stuff, Sheryl. I told my mother I threw it all away. I got sick of her putting me down all the time, making fun of me wanting to be an artist. It's like she was jealous or something. What a bummer."

Sheryl put her arm around Emma's shoulder. "It's cool darlin'. I'm your friend. What else could I do?"

They spread the quilt on the ground and sat down. Emma pulled out her charcoal pencils while Sheryl lit up a Tareyton.

"How can you smoke those things?"

"I got the habit, girl, and I can't kick it."

Emma looked around. There were a few people in the park. Sitting at a table close to them was a young Amish man. He was dark-haired and rugged-looking. Strong arms and a powerful chest filled his shirt, and he had a chiseled, striking face.

"Look at that guy," Emma whispered. "What a hunk."

"You like everything Amish."

"Why shouldn't I? That's who I am. Just because my mother got kicked out doesn't mean I can't find out about them. My grandparents came from Germany. The Amish go back to the middle ages over there. It's my history, it's who I am."

"Well, your mom sure hates it when you ask about them."

Emma looked away. "My mom... she's just weird."

"Why don't you go ask him if you can draw him?"

Emma looked at Sheryl. "Should I?"

"Why not? He can only say no."

Emma got up and walked over to the table. The young man looked up. He smiled at Emma. "*Guten Abend,*" he said, and lifted his hat.

"That means 'good evening,' right?"

He smiled and nodded. "*Ja,* good evening."

Emma looked down, suddenly shy. She hesitated, but she was here, so she took a breath. "Can I draw you?" she blurted out.

"Are you an artist?"

"Yes... I mean, no... Well, yes. I am an artist." She looked down again. "At least I want to be," she whispered.

He looked at her for a long time, then smiled again. For a minute Emma thought the sun had broken through and bathed his face with light.

"You have a very... striking face. I want to capture it... I mean... in a picture." She blushed.

The young man nodded. "*Ja,* okay. What do you want me to do?"

"Just sit. Let me look at you. Try to hold still. These are just sketches, so it won't take long."

She sat staring at his face.

"Well, are you going to draw?" He smiled.

Emma turned beet red. She picked up her pencil and began sketching...

∽

Jacob looked over at Elbert. "And that is how we met. When Dennis came back a few hours later to pick them up, she asked if she could sketch me again. I said yes, and we set a time. I was in *Rumspringa*, so I could do what I wanted, go where I wanted. My parents didn't question me. She got Dennis to bring her the next time we met. Dennis became our 'go-between.' He helped us. Even Sheryl didn't know we were meeting, because Emma was so afraid of her mama. And she didn't want Sheryl jealous. I would buy some wine and give it to him. It was a good deal."

Elbert tapped his pencil on the desk. "So, you started seeing each other regularly?"

"*Ja*. Dennis would bring her to the park, and I would take her in my buggy. It was harvest time, and I took her out to the fields where the men were working. The Amish fascinated her. She drew the men, the machines, the horses. She drew the women helping in the fields..."

Jacob's voice cracked. "She was such a wonderful artist. She... She..."

He put his face down in his arms on the table and wept. "Oh, Emma, Emma, I am so sorry, *ich wollte dich niemals verletzen...*"

"Jacob, do you need a drink of water?"

Jacob lifted his head and waved the glass away. "*Nein*, go ahead."

Elbert pushed a box of Kleenex over to Jacob's side of the table. "What happened after that?"

"What happened? I fell in love with her and she fell in love with me. We became... *Liebhaber*, lovers. I wanted her to marry me, but she was afraid, so afraid of her mama."

"Okay, tell me about the night Emma was killed."

Jacob's face paled, but he nodded.

"I had the ring I made for her. Dennis brought her to my father's shop, then he left. My papa and mama were away, visiting friends for a few days. We had some wine. We drank too much. Both of us were a little woozy. We were under the quilt. I got up and got the ring, showed it to her. Put it on her finger. She... she..."

"What happened then, Jacob?"

"She... changed."

∼

EMMA LOOKED DOWN at the ring on her finger. Something tightened in her insides... fear. She pulled the quilt around her and stood up. Her head was spinning. She staggered and then she held her hand up. The golden ring glowed in the lantern light and she laughed. Jacob looked at her with pain in his eyes.

"Why are you laughing?"

Emma waved the ring in his face. "I suppose you think this means we are engaged. Well, it doesn't. I can't marry you. I can never marry an Amish. My mother would kill me."

Jacob loomed over her. "Give it back, then!"

"No! It's mine. You gave it to me. I'll keep it as a memento of a fun time."

Jacob's face twisted. "Fun time? Fun time? Is that all you think? After what we've been to each other? Give it back, I say!"

Jacob grabbed her hand and pulled, but she twisted out of his grip and he stumbled, striking his head on the table. He fell to the floor and lay still.

Emma dropped to her knees beside him and tried to wake him. "Jacob, wake up. I'm sorry. I'll marry you, I love you..."

∼

JACOB WIPED HIS EYES. He looked at Elbert. "When I hit my head, I blacked out. I don't remember what happened next. When I woke up, I had a hammer in my hand. Emma was lying there, still wrapped in the quilt. Her head was bloody. There was blood on the hammer. She was..."

"Dead, Jacob?"

Jacob nodded slowly. "Yes. Emma was dead."

"What did you do then?"

"I panicked. I knew if I told anyone or anyone found out, I would go to prison or they would put me in the electric chair. There was a box in the storeroom, part of the cabinet my father made. I wrapped her in the quilt and put her in the box. Jepson's woods are right across the road. I put the box in a handcart and wheeled her over to the woods. She weighed nothing at all. She was so light. It was late, nobody was around. I found a place in the woods and buried her."

"You left the ring on her hand."

"*Ja*, I wasn't thinking. I remembered it later, but it was too late. And now the quilt and the ring have found me out."

"Why did you use the box? Why didn't you just bury her?"

Jacob lifted his head. "I am Amish. Emma was Amish in her heart. We do not just throw our people in a hole in the ground."

"What did you do then?"

"Her clothes were still at the shop. I gathered them up and burned them. When my father came home a few days later, I told him someone broke into the shop and stole the cabinet."

Elbert nodded at the officer. "Okay, I think we have enough. Jacob, I will have a copy of your confession drawn up. Will you sign it?"

Jacob nodded. He looked at Elbert and sighed. "I am just glad it is finally over."

"I will need to talk to you about Dennis and Gary."

Jacob shook his head. "Dennis was my friend. He helped me by driving Emma to meet me. I liked him a lot. I did not kill him and I do not even know who this Gary is."

"That's your story?"

Jacob nodded.

"Okay, officer. You can take him back."

In the room next door, Jenny looked at Bobby. "Jacob did not kill Emma, or Dennis or Gary."

"What?"

"He is not the killer, and I think I know who is. I just have to prove it."

21

CASE CLOSED?

"So, they caught the monster who killed my Emma, did they? And it was an Amish man? Sure, who else would it be? The Amish are all phonies and liars. The only one I ever met that was honest was your mother, Jenny. And even she had to hide the fact that she was still my friend." She saw Jenny's frown. "Oh, I'm sorry. You seem to be a decent sort too, Jenny." She smiled. "Nosey, but decent."

"I know you had a terrible experience when you were young, Chantrice, but you shouldn't let that sour you on all the Amish. A very wicked Amish *bisschopf* caused my mama and papa's deaths. But it had nothing to do with the fact he was Amish and everything to do with the fact he was an evil, evil person. When it happened, the Amish stood up to him and made him be accountable for his actions. He was in jail here for a long time and then they sent him back to Pennsylvania and he died in jail there."

"I'm sorry, Jenny. I just wish the Amish stood up for me like they did for you, when I had my trouble. But they didn't. They threw me out."

"Yes, I know. And I was under the *meidung* too. I know how it feels."

Chantrice looked surprised. "You?"

"Yes. I wanted to marry an *englischer*. I was going to run away. My papa did what he believed was right."

"But you don't know... Oh, never mind."

"Know what, Chantrice?"

"What I went through was horrible, but it doesn't matter now, Jenny. I'm not Amish anymore, and I haven't been for almost fifty years. Too much water under the bridge to even worry about it." She sat and motioned Jenny to sit next to her. "Tell me about the murderer."

Jenny nodded. "His name is Jacob Troyer. Sheryl Krantz said Emma met him when he was in *Rumspringa*. She started sketching him and I guess they fell in love."

"He was the one she was sleeping with, then?"

"Yes."

"I knew it. I knew she was up to something when I found the birth control things in her drawer. The Amish. They are just like everybody else. They act so holy and they are just as perverted as everyone else."

Jenny stood up. "Chantrice, I came here to tell you what happened. If you cannot refrain from attacking my people, I will leave now and send Bobby and Elbert to talk with you."

Chantrice grabbed Jenny's arm. "Please, don't go. I'm sorry, Jenny. I won't say another word. This whole thing is horrible. It's got me all worked up. I need a cigarette."

"Do you mind if we go outside, Chantrice?"

"Not at all. We can sit on the porch."

The two women went outside and sat in the porch's shade. It was a sunny day, but the chill of autumn was in the air. Fall smells drifted in the breeze; cornstalks burning in gardens, dying leaves composting in their piles; smells that usually filled Jenny's thoughts with glad visions, but today, she could only think about Emma.

Chantrice lit a cigarette and inhaled deeply. "Ah, that's better.

I know I shouldn't smoke, but it relaxes me. Now tell me what happened, Jenny. I won't say another word."

Jenny nodded. "Okay, Chantrice. It seems that Jacob Troyer and Emma fell in love after Emma started sketching him. They spent a lot of time together. Jacob says that Emma was fascinated by all things Amish. She made him take her out to the fields where she sketched the Amish men working in the fields, horses, the wagons and equipment, women working beside the men."

Chantrice was silent for a long moment. "I used to love the harvest. The men working together, singing at the end of day, *Das Lobleid...*" she paused. "Go on, what happened?"

"The night Emma was killed, they were together in the Troyer workshop. Jacob's parents were gone, and they were alone. They had been drinking and Jacob said they were drunk or close to it. He had a ring that he bought for Emma. He gave it to her, asked her to marry him."

"What did she do?"

"Jacob said she laughed at him. Told him if he thought they were engaged, he was very wrong. She said that you would kill her before you let her marry an Amish man."

Chantrice took another drag. "That's a little strong, I think. But of course, I would never have allowed it."

"Anyway, Jacob asked her to give the ring back. She refused, said he had given it to her and she would keep it as a memento. Jacob tried to grab it, but she twisted away. He fell and hit his head. When he woke up, Emma was dead, and he had one of his father's mallets in his hand. The mallet was covered with blood. He says he doesn't remember killing her."

Chantrice shook her head. "A likely story. He's just trying to get off. Oh, he did it all right, and I bet that is just a story he made up to get sympathy."

Jenny went on. "When he realized she was dead, he wrapped her in the quilt. Put her in one of his father's cabinets, wheeled her across the road to Jepson's woods and buried her. When he was back home, he realized the ring was still on her finger, but there was nothing he could do about it. So, he's been living in fear and guilt ever since."

Chantrice snickered. "Funny how things turn out, isn't it? The quilt and the ring found him out after all this time. The quilt that knew." She took another drag. "The guilty never escape, do they? Isn't there a Bible verse that says your sin will find you out?"

"Yes, there are quite a few. In Galatians, it says, 'Do not be deceived: God is not mocked, for whatever one sows, that will he also reap.' And in Luke it says, 'For nothing is hidden that will not be made manifest, nor is anything secret that will not be known and come to light.'"

"What about Dennis Cummings?"

"What about him?"

"Did Jacob Troyer confess to that too? It was in the paper they charged him with three murders."

"He says he didn't kill Dennis. The police are working on that."

Chantrice looked long and hard at Jenny, then stubbed out her cigarette and flipped the butt off the porch. "Thank you for coming, Jenny. I'm glad you helped solve this mystery. I need to go in and lie down now. This whole thing has just set me all a'twitter. Keep me informed, would you?"

Jenny took her hand and pulled her into a hug. "My mama loved you, Chantrice. She wouldn't have made that quilt for you if she didn't." She stepped back. Chantrice looked at Jenny and there were tears in her eyes. "I loved your mama, too. She was the only person in my whole life who was ever good to me." She turned and went into the house.

When the door closed, Jenny walked down the steps. As she was walking, she pulled a small plastic bag and a cue tip from her pocket, bent down on the sidewalk and nudged something into the bag.

"So, it was Emma's Amish lover all the time?" Sheryl Krantz looked at Jenny and shook her head.

"Yes, Sheryl, but I have something else to tell you. It's not good news."

Sheryl's eyes opened wide. "What? Is it about Dennis?"

"Yes. He... he is dead, Sheryl."

Sheryl turned white and then red and then white again. "Dead? But how, when?" Her hands went to her mouth.

"They found Dennis's car in a wild area outside Wooster. It was buried in a deep gully for almost the same amount of time that Emma was buried."

"You mean Dennis never left?"

"No, Sheryl, he never left. He was killed about the same time as Emma, probably by the same person."

"You mean Jacob Troyer?"

"Maybe. Someone lured him up to the woods, hit him in the head with a mallet, and then drove his car over a cliff. He's been there all this time."

Sheryl gave a small smile and murmured. "He didn't leave me. All these years, I thought he and Emma betrayed me. But they didn't." She put her hands to her heart. "Oh, he loved me. He didn't leave me. Dennis, Dennis..."

Sheryl put her hands to her face and burst into tears. Jenny moved close and comforted her while she wept and wept. Finally, she stopped. Jenny handed her a hanky, and she wiped her eyes and blew her nose. When she was done, she handed the hanky back to Jenny.

Jenny looked at the small watch in her purse. "I have to go if I want to catch the bus. I'm sorry about Dennis."

"Don't be sorry. I know it never would have worked between us, especially after I met the Lord. I'm content to know that he did not betray me, that he loved me. That will keep me until the day I die."

She rose and Jenny stood up and took her into her arms. "Sheryl, the Lord bless you, and keep you; The Lord cause His face to shine on you, and be gracious to you; The Lord lift up His face to you, and give you peace."

Jenny hugged Sheryl. She hugged Jenny back.

"Thank you, Jenny, for all you've done."

"Can I ask you one more thing, Sheryl?"

"Anything."

"If I need your help clearing up some of the last details in this case, can I call on you?"

"Anytime, just call." Then Sheryl turned and walked into the house.

Jenny slipped the hanky into a plastic bag in her purse and walked down the steps.

~

Jenny sat with Elbert and Bobby in the evidence room at the police station. She looked over at Elbert. "When we looked at the hair in Emma's comb and compared it to Emma's hair, what kind of analysis did we run?"

Elbert shrugged. "We did a simple comparison. The two hair strands were not from the same person."

"Would a DNA test be more revealing?"

Elbert nodded. "Oh, yes. DNA would be a much more detailed analysis. We could analyze the hair samples and then compare them with DNA samples in our database. If the person is in the database or even a relative, we can pin down their identity."

"And you can tell if the different hair strands are related somehow?"

"Absolutely."

Bobby grinned. "What are you getting at, Jenny? I can see your mind working."

Jenny smiled back. "I have felt all along that there is something wrong with this case. Finding Jacob Troyer was too easy. It was almost as if someone set him up. I watched his face when you accused him of murdering Dennis Cummings and he was genuinely surprised. I believe there was somebody else there that night and I think I know who it was."

"So, what do you want to do, Jenny?" Bobby asked.

Jenny pulled two plastic bags from her pocket and put them on the table. Then she reached in her purse and took out the fish charm. "I found this charm in a crack in the floor at the Troyer shop. Sheryl Krantz told me that Emma had only two things she really loved—her quilt and her fish charm bracelet. She was never without them. I saw someone wearing a fish charm bracelet that was missing one piece. I think this is the piece, and I think the person who has the bracelet took it from Emma after killing her."

Elbert looked at Bobby and then back at Jenny. "Okay, what's the next step?"

"I want you to run a DNA test on the hair sample from the brush, and the hair sample from the body, and I want you to compare them with the DNA on what's in these bags. One of them is a test, one is from the person I believe is our killer. Be sure and check for fingerprints and DNA. When you find out the results, if they are what I think they are, then you need to get a search warrant for this address."

Jenny pushed a piece of paper over to Elbert and Bobby. Bobby picked it up. He looked at it and his eyes opened in surprise. He handed it to Elbert.

"Whew. Really?"

Jenny nodded. "If you need me to testify for the search warrant, I will testify that I saw this person wearing the charm bracelet. I also think you should put my mama's box down as one item you are searching for because I think you will find it there. If I am right, the fingerprints you find and the DNA will confirm everything."

"Man, oh man, Jenny. If you are right about this, we were as far as the East is from the West on this case."

"What made me think about this was remembering when I first met Jonathan. He looked and acted a certain way, and that kept me from seeing who he really was. If I am right, this person has been cleverly misdirecting us the whole time. The answer has been right in front of us and we didn't see it. The worst is so often true."

22
THE LITTLEST THINGS

Fred Granger, the technician in charge of the laboratory that did DNA sampling and forensics for the Wooster Police Department, stared at the samples through the electron microscope. Elbert had submitted hair from a brush and the girl in the box. He had two strands, one of each, under the microscope and he examined them side by side. It was obvious they were not from the same person. He looked at Elbert, who was sitting across the lab table.

"The hair from the corpse has no follicle, which contains the cell nucleus, because the mummification process destroyed it after the girl died. The hair on the brush has a follicle, but… it has degraded too."

Elbert frowned. "Does that mean we can't find DNA?"

"Not at all. It just prohibits us from running a test for nuclear DNA to prove paternity. We can still run a mitochondrial test and then compare the results of that. In fact, it will give us a much more complete result and we can use for it comparison with the other items. It is, however, a complex process and will take me more than an afternoon."

"When can you have it?"

Fred glanced over at his wall calendar. "Today is Tuesday... how about Thursday afternoon?"

"Can you have it Wednesday afternoon? And can you check the mallet, the cigarette and the hanky for DNA as well? This is a big deal."

Fred sighed. "Okay, okay. It's always a big deal, but I'll work late."

"Thanks, Fred. I owe you."

Elbert walked out.

∼

WEDNESDAY AFTERNOON, he was back in the lab. Fred had the analysis spread out on the desk.

"Here are the results, Elbert."

Elbert pulled up a chair and scanned the report. As he did, his eyes widened. He looked over at Fred. "You sure you got this right?"

Fred shook his head. "How long have you been working with me, Detective?"

"Quite a few years."

"Ever known me to miss?"

"No."

"Elbert, what you have there is the complete genetic examination of the person whose hair was in the comb and the person who was in the box. And you are in luck. There are two fingerprints on the mallet. The blood from the victims ran down the handle and the killer left a very complete print and a partial print in it."

"Victims?"

"Yes. The mallet had Emma Johnson's DNA on it, too. I also checked for fingerprints and DNA on the cigarette butt and the hanky. There was a match. And the summation you have is what it shows."

Elbert put the report back in its folder and stood up. "Wait until Jenny and Bobby see this."

∼

Bobby looked up from the report. "Wow, talk about blindsided. What are we going to do with this?"

Jenny looked over at Elbert. "I would like to get the main characters in this play together down here. I would like to... I guess you would call it interview them. And then I would like to share the results of our test with them. While they are here, that is when you should execute the search warrant you will get. How fast can you arrange that?"

"I can have one by this afternoon. Did you sign your affidavit?"

"Yes. That and the matching fingerprints should give you carte blanche with a judge."

Jenny reread a section of the report. She pointed to it. "And right here is the answer to all the questions we have had about this case."

∼

Jenny was sitting on one side of a long table in the station's interview room. She had a small box and two manila folders on the table in front of her. She was studying the contents of one folder. When Sheryl Krantz came in, she glanced up.

"Thank you for coming, Sheryl."

"I said I would help you in whatever way I could."

"Good. When everyone arrives, I am going to ask some hard questions. Please bear with me. In the end, we will make everything clear."

"Well, well. Sheryl Krantz. I thought you moved away a long time ago."

Jenny and Sheryl turned. Chantrice Edwards stood in the doorway.

Sheryl's face hardened and Jenny noticed.

"Hello, Mrs. Edwards. No, I never left. I live in my parents' old house. I've been there for over thirty years. How have you been?"

"Oh, you know. Middlin'. Life changed after Emma left. But you know that." She turned to Jenny. "So why have you asked me here? You have the killer. Shouldn't you be concentrating on him?"

Jenny motioned to some chairs that were set up on the opposite side of the table from her.

"Well, Chantrice, we have a few details to take care of and I've asked everyone concerned with the case to come in. If you will take a chair, we have one more person we are waiting for, and then we can get started."

Chantrice looked around. "Who else is coming?"

A door on the far side of the room opened and a deputy sheriff came in. "Are you ready for him, ma'am?"

Jenny nodded. "Yes, Deputy, I am. Bring him in."

The deputy motioned through the open door to someone outside. Jacob Troyer came into the room. He wore an orange jumpsuit and had manacles on his wrists. Jenny motioned to a chair at the end of the table, and Jacob sat down.

"You can take those manacles off, Deputy. I don't think Jacob is a danger to us."

"Yes, ma'am, but I will have to stay in the room."

"That's fine, Deputy. There's a chair right against the wall."

The deputy unlocked the cuffs and Jacob sat down. He looked at Jenny gratefully as he rubbed his wrists. "*Danke*, Jenny."

"What's he doing here? He murdered my baby. I won't stay in the same room with him." Chantrice stood up.

"Please, sit down, Chantrice!" There was strong authority in Jenny's voice, and Chantrice slowly sank back into her chair.

Jenny looked at the three people. "Some things have come up

that we were not aware of when Jacob was arrested, some things that have shed a whole new light on this case."

She paused and looked at each person.

"We believe that someone else was there when Emma was killed. In fact, we know they were."

She looked at the faces of the people in front of her. Jacob's mouth was open in amazement.

"But there was no one else."

"We believe they came in while you were unconscious. We also believe that this person is the one who committed the murder."

She could see the amazement on Jacob and Sheryl's face. Chantrice looked at her with burning eyes.

"I have a few questions for each of you, and depending on what the answers are, I believe we can wrap this case up today." She turned to Jacob. "Let's start with you, Jacob. What happened when you struggled with Emma, when you were trying to take the ring back? Tell me everything you remember."

"Emma laughed at me. She said she could never marry me. She said her mother would kill her if she ever married an Amish man."

"Go on."

"I asked for the ring back. She wouldn't give it to me. Said it would be a reminder of all the fun we had. Fun? It was just fun to her? I was drunk and what she said made me *sehr wütend*. She twisted out of my grip when I tried to grab the ring and I fell. I hit my head on the table's edge. That's all I remember until I came to. She was lying there. The back of her head was all bloody. I had a bloody mallet in my hand."

"What did you do with that mallet?"

"I threw it in the pond."

"Did your father have other mallets?"

"Oh, yes, he had many. He needed different weights for precision work."

Jenny reached into a bag beside her chair and pulled out something in a plastic bag. "Do you recognize this?"

Jacob looked startled. "Yes, that is one of my father's mallets. It should have the initials J.T. carved on the back. Where did you get that?"

Jenny showed Jacob the initials. "This is the weapon that killed Dennis Cummings. We believe it is also the mallet that was used to kill Emma. The police found it in Dennis's car, along with his remains. It has traces of Emma's blood on it."

Jacob stared at the mallet. "But it can't be. I threw the mallet I killed Emma with in the pond."

"You just thought you threw away the murder weapon. But we'll get to that."

She turned to Sheryl. "Sheryl, what do you remember about the night Dennis left? Are there any details you can think of that you didn't already share with me?"

Sheryl thought for a moment. "Let's see. He came by my house about six o'clock. He was behaving strangely, not his usual joking self. He was quiet, said he had found a way for us to go to San Francisco. He was getting some money. I asked him how he could do that." She paused and then she turned to Jenny. "He said he was getting the money from someone that he knew something about. Someone who was willing to pay him to go away. I asked him if that wasn't blackmail. He said it kind of was, but it was our big chance. Something had happened, and he just wanted to get away, forever—and take me with him."

Jenny looked directly at Sheryl. "Did you know he was seeing Emma without you? That two or three times a week, he would go to her house and she would sneak out to meet him."

Jenny glanced at Chantrice. The woman's face was hard and cold and she leaned forward to hear Sheryl's answer.

"Did you?"

Sheryl nodded. "Yes, I suspected.... But I couldn't believe they were cheating on me."

"Did you have a car back then?"

"Yes, my parents let me use theirs sometimes."

"When you suspected they were betraying you, did you ever follow them in your parent's car?"

Sheryl turned pale. She nodded. "Yes. One night I followed them. They drove out toward Jepson's woods. They turned down a lane. I left my car out on the road and walked down a little way. I saw them get out and go into a building. I was going to confront them, but I couldn't do it. I guess I didn't want to know the truth. So I turned around and went home. Then the next day, he came by like nothing happened and told me he was going to California. He wanted me to come with him. I didn't know what to think, but I got ready anyway."

"So, when you were out that night and watched them go into the building together, you didn't go inside?"

"No."

"Yes, you did," said Chantrice. She turned to Jenny. "Don't you see? If you think someone else was there, someone who killed Emma while Jacob was unconscious, it must be her. Emma was sneaking around with her boyfriend. She followed them and when Dennis left, she went inside and killed Emma. Jealousy, Jenny, is a powerful motivator."

Sheryl looked from Chantrice to Jenny. "I didn't go in, I swear. I went home. The next day, Dennis came by, told me to get ready to go. But then they both disappeared. I thought he had changed his mind and taken Emma instead. All these years, I thought he changed his mind..."

Chantrice almost hissed. "You're a liar." She pointed at Sheryl. "I tell you, it was her."

Jenny interrupted. "When did Dennis come to your house, Sheryl, to tell you about getting some money?"

"The very next day, around noon."

"Thank you."

Just then, the door opened and Elbert and Bobby came in.

Elbert had a cardboard box under his arm. Bobby was carrying something else. It was Jerusha's quilting box. Jenny's heart leaped. She looked at Chantrice. The woman's face had gone white.

"Did you find everything you were looking for?"

"Yes. And a lot more, just like you thought." He handed Jenny the box. Bobby sat next to Jenny and placed Jerusha's box next to him.

Jenny opened Elbert's box, looked inside, took out something, and laid it on the table in front of Chantrice. Sheryl gasped. Chantrice started to stand up.

"Chantrice, do you recognize this?"

But Sheryl spoke first. "That's Emma's bracelet. Where did you find it?"

Jenny looked at Chantrice. "Where did I find it, Chantrice?"

"How in the world would I know?"

"Detective Wainwright found this box in the crawl space of your house."

Chantrice was standing now. "What was he doing in my house?"

Elbert sat on the other side of Jenny. "I had a search warrant, Mrs. Edwards. I got the search warrant because I have proof that you were involved in the killing of Emma Johnson and Dennis Cummings."

"What are you talking about?"

"Tell her, Jenny."

Jenny reached into the small evidence box in front of her and brought out the single fish charm. She showed it to Chantrice. "Do you recognize this?"

"I've never seen it." There was desperation in her voice.

"Yes, you have, Chantrice, many times. On Emma's wrist. Do you know where I found it?"

"I don't have the slightest…"

"I found it in Jacob's shop. It was under a pile of sawdust. It had been there a long time. The only way it could have gotten there is if it broke off when the killer tore the bracelet off Emma's wrist. But that was your mistake. You couldn't just leave the bracelet on her, you had to have it. After all, it's pure silver. Emma worked for a long time to earn the money to buy it. And once when I was at your house, I saw you wearing that bracelet. You didn't think anyone would know it was Emma's. After all, Dennis was dead. Sheryl was probably long gone. And that was your mistake."

"You're a liar, Jenny Hershberger."

"No, Chantrice. I'm not. And there is something else. We examined the hairs in the brush. I have always felt someone was deliberately trying to mislead us. I was right. You took Emma's hair out of the brush and then brushed your hair with it. You thought we would just compare them and think the hair in the brush was Emma's and it wouldn't match the dead girl's hair. You didn't know we would run a DNA test on them. But we did, and we found out something. Because we also had a cigarette butt I collected off your sidewalk to check your DNA against. You know what we found? We found out the reason you hate the Amish and the reason you hated Emma."

Chantrice was sweating, looking around. "What is that, pray tell?"

"You and Emma shared a great deal more DNA than a mother and daughter normally would. You both had 50% of the father's DNA. But it was the same DNA in both of you. Emma was your daughter, yes. But she was also your sister!"

23
THE QUILT THAT KNEW

Chantrice Edwards rose from her chair. Her face was white with fury and her fingers clutched at the air in front of her.

"What do you mean, she's my sister?" she screamed!

Jenny spoke softly. "Something dreadful happened to you when you were young, something that my mother knew about. That's why she made the quilt for you."

"I don't know what you are talking about," Chantrice hissed.

"You know what I'm talking about, Chantrice. It was your father. Your father was also Emma's father. The DNA tests prove it conclusively. You both share the same DNA on the father's side."

Chantrice looked around frantically, and then she bolted toward the door. But the deputy who was there, blocked her. Her arms dropped, and she turned slowly to Jenny. "You meddling fool! Why did you come back here?"

She advanced to the table and put her hands on it. She leaned over until she was face to face with Jenny. "Yes, my father was Emma's father. When I was thirteen, he started coming to my room almost every night. My mother knew, but she did nothing. She just pretended it wasn't happening. That arrogant pig.

During the day he was walking around, acting holy, hobnobbing with the *bisschopf* and then at night he was raping me."

Jenny nodded. "And then you got pregnant."

"Yes. I was sixteen. I went to my mother and told her I was going to tell everyone who the father was. But he acted first. He went to the elders and told them I was pregnant by an *Englischer*. He paid Merrill a lot of money, got him to say he was the father, got him a job in the mill. Then he had the elders throw me out."

"You could have gotten a paternity test when Emma was born. You could have proved he was the father."

Chantrice's face tightened. "Yeah, except the miserable coward died. He had a stroke and died before Emma was born. He was dead and buried. There was no way to prove anything. Jerusha knew, but what could she do? My father had thrown me out. I had nothing. So, I married Merrill. At least he took care of me. He was nice enough, a kind man. But I couldn't take revenge on my father. I couldn't take revenge on any of them."

"So, you've hated all Amish ever since."

"Yes."

"What happened that night? The night Emma died."

Chantrice sank into her chair. "I knew she was seeing an Amish man. She loved everything Amish. It made me sick to my stomach. I saw some of her drawings. The man she kept drawing —I could tell she loved him. I told her she was a fool for having anything to do with him. I told her to stop bringing that trash in the house. The drawings disappeared. She told me she tore them up, that she was done with him."

Sheryl spoke up. "But she didn't tear them up, Mrs. Edwards, she gave them to me. And she didn't stop seeing Jacob."

Chantrice nodded. "No, she didn't. And when I found the birth control, I knew she had lied to me."

Jenny nodded. "So, when Dennis came for her that night and she snuck out, you followed her."

"Yes. He drove her to the Troyer shop. Then he left. I waited. I watched through the window. They drank wine. Then they, they... they got under the quilt. After a while, Jacob got up and got the ring. He put it on her finger. She laughed at him, told him she couldn't marry him, that I would kill her if she did."

Jenny pushed ahead. "And she was right, wasn't she?"

"They fought over the ring. He fell and hit his head. She was down on her knees telling him to wake up, that she loved him, that she would marry him."

Jacob's face went pale. "She said that?"

Chantrice looked at him with pure venom on her face. "Yes, you fool. She loved you."

"You went in?" Jenny asked, quietly.

"Yes! Yes! I went in. There was a mallet on the table. She was kneeling at his side. She kept saying she would marry him, begging him to wake up. She kept saying she loved him. Over and over. I came up behind her."

"She heard you?"

"Yes! She looked up at me. I told her she would never marry an Amish man. She said she would and I couldn't stop her. And then I hit her, again, and again, and again."

"Then what happened?" Elbert asked.

"When I finished, she was lying there. The devil's spawn was dead."

"You finally got your revenge. You took it out on Emma."

"Yes! Yes! My revenge! From the time she was born, every time I looked at her I remembered his groping hands, his stinking breath, his lies, how he kept telling me if people loved each other, this is what they did."

"Then what did you do?"

"Jacob was still unconscious. My fingerprints were on the mallet, so I got another, put her blood on it and put it in his hand." She pointed at Jacob. "I thought they would catch him, that they would put him in prison. But he put her in the box and buried her. All these years Emma was in the box in the ground. If those boys hadn't found her, you never would have come back here." She looked around.

"At first, after it happened, I wanted them to catch him. They would have put him in the electric chair. But a quick death was too good for him. I realized he was in his own hell. He believed he murdered the girl he loved. Oh, how I used to laugh when I thought of him suffering, tormented, wanting to die but too much of a coward to kill himself."

Chantrice got a strange look in her eyes and she spoke again, almost to herself. "It was only fair that he suffered like I suffered. It gave me peace thinking about it. He deserved to suffer the torment of the damned because... because..."

Jenny leaned forward. "Because he's Amish?"

A look of pure hatred came over Chantrice's face. "Yes, because he's Amish! He's Amish. May they all be forever damned! Emma is dead because of him, because of them! The Amish. What hypocrites! Everybody thinks they are wonderful Christian people, rustic, peace-loving farmers that live off the land. But you know what? They all deserve to suffer, to die. I tried to tell them what my father was, what he did, but they would not listen. After all, he was an important man, he had money, he ran the mill. I was just a young girl. What was I in their grand world? Nothing! I was nothing! He made them think I was crazy. And my mother..." she spit on the floor. "My mother could have protected me, could have saved me from him. But she was weak. He terrorized her, and so she turned a blind eye. I needed her so, but she wouldn't help me. She was just as evil as they were. Yes, I hate them, I hate them all." She looked at Jenny. There was malevolence in her eyes. "And especially you, you meddling, arrogant clown. The great Jenny Hershberger, the famous Amish writer. What a joke!" Suddenly, she lunged across the table at Jenny, screaming. "I'll kill you, I'll kill you too!" But before she could reach Jenny, she was in the steel grip of Bobby Halverson. She struggled, but Bobby held her until she stopped.

"Not a good thing to try, Chantrice." Bobby nodded to the detective. "Elbert?"

Elbert came around the table. He pulled Chantrice's hands behind her back and slipped a pair of handcuffs on them. "Chantrice Edwards, I am arresting you for the murders of Emma Johnson, Dennis Cummings, and Gary Walker. You have the right to remain silent. Anything you say can be used against you in court. You have the right to talk to a lawyer for advice before we ask you any questions. You have the right to have a lawyer with you during questioning..."

~

THE NEXT DAY, Elbert called Jenny and asked her and Bobby to come to the station. When they got there, he was waiting in the lobby with several Amish men and women, including the *bisschopf*. They all looked up when Jenny entered. The *bisschopf* extended his hand. "We want to thank you for solving this mystery. We have heard the story and we are ashamed. This never should have happened in our community. We are going to speak with Chantrice. Will you come?"

Jenny nodded. "I'm not sure what her response will be."

"We are willing to try."

Bobby looked at Jenny. "I'll wait here. This is none of my business."

Elbert took them down the hall to a holding cell. Chantrice Edwards was sitting on the bunk, staring at the wall. She heard footsteps and turned. Her face went white when she saw the group of Amish that gathered in the hall. She got up and came to the bars. She stared at them. Finally, she spoke.

"What do you want? Did you come to mock me, torment me, tell me how horrible I am?"

The *bisschopf* shook his head. "No, Chantrice, we have not come to mock. We have come to humble ourselves. What happened to you should never have happened. We Amish pride ourselves in trying to be fair and honest in all our dealings. We try to follow Jesus's commandments at all times. But we did not do that when you needed us. Our eyes were blinded, and we did not hear the cry for help from a young girl who deserved just as much of our ear as a wealthy mill owner."

"What are you saying?"

The *bisschopf* took off his hat. "We are here to beg your forgiveness. If we had been who we say we are, you would still be part of us, one of our daughters. It would have been your father the elders shunned. But they failed, so we all failed. We failed you, we failed our church and especially we failed Jesus. You told the truth, and no one believed you except Jerusha Springer. Now you are here and for that we are so sorry. Will you forgive us?"

Chantrice looked at them for a long time. Tears ran down her cheeks. She sighed and shook her head. "No, I cannot." She turned away.

The *bisschopf* stepped closer. "Perhaps in time you will see..."

Chantrice turned back. "No, maybe in time you will see! Don't you understand? Being Amish made me very happy, it was who I was. I never wanted to be anything else. I loved going to the fields to watch the men at harvest. I loved the animals in the barn, I loved the land, the church, I loved singing the hymns, *das Lobleid*... When you took that away from me, I became nothing. You took my identity away and left me the bitter waters of Marah. Every day when I woke, there was nothing, just emptiness stretching away into a darkness that loomed before me in all my waking moments. No, I cannot forgive you because there is nobody inside me who can forgive. Chantrice Stoltzfus died fifty years ago." She pointed to herself. "This is what you left. Now go, please..."

The Amish people slowly walked away. Jenny stayed for a moment. "I told you before, Chantrice, and I will tell you again.

My mama loved you very much. She prayed for you, I remember."

Chantrice's answer came back, muffled, quiet. "It didn't help."

∼

Jenny went back out to the front. Elbert stopped her. "Jacob Troyer wants to speak to you."

He took her back to Jacob's cell. Jacob stood up when he saw her and came to the bars. "I want to thank you, Jenny. For forty years I have been in torment every day, horrible agony, thinking that I killed the only girl I ever loved. To hear from her mother's lips that she was begging me to wake up, that she loved me, she would marry me... that has delivered my soul. I can live the rest of my life in peace. *Danke, danke von ganzem Herzen.*" He reached through the bars and took her hand, held it for a moment, and then let her go.

Jenny walked back down the hall. She lifted her eyes.

Danke mein liebender Gott, dass du mir geholfen hast.

24
GOING HOME

*J*enny, Bobby, Rachel, Daniel, and Elbert sat at the table in a very nice restaurant in Wooster. Rachel looked at her mother admiringly. "Mama, how did you figure all this out?"

Jenny put down her fork. "It all came from the conversation we had about crimes that are committed in small villages, and how we always overlook the most obvious things. People commit crimes for the same reasons—money, sex or power—no matter where they live. And we talked about how, in a village like Apple creek, crimes usually are perpetrated by someone who is right under your nose, someone you would never suspect."

"So, in Chantrice's case..."

"In her case, the sexual abuse by her father destroyed her life. What started this whole horrible saga was a local crime perpetrated by a well-respected local man. That crime put a hatred in her heart that she could not overcome."

Rachel nodded. "So, because of that, every time Chantrice looked at Emma, it reminded her of her father, and she felt the fear and the terror of his nightly visits all over again?"

"Yes," Jenny agreed.

Rachel shook her head. "How terrible… and sad. And to think it all happened right here, in Apple Creek, from the first crime sixty years ago, to the murder of Emma and Dennis and finally to the death of Gary Walker."

Bobby chimed in. "Because of her loathing for her father and the Amish community, the thought of her daughter going back to the Amish was more than she could bear. And when she came in that night at the Troyer's, and heard Emma telling Jacob she loved him, that she would marry him…"

"It put her over the edge," said Daniel, "And she killed Emma."

"Exactly," answered Jenny. "Then she compounded the crime by killing Dennis and years later, Gary."

"What about Dennis Cummings, Mama? Why was he killed?"

"From what Chantrice told Elbert, and from what we know from Sheryl, Dennis came back early to pick up Emma. He heard Chantrice screaming at Emma—that she would never marry an Amish man. He looked in the window just in time to see Chantrice kill Emma. Dennis watched as she smeared Emma's blood on a mallet and put it in Jacob's hand. At that point, he ran away. But later, in a calmer moment, he decided this would be a chance to get enough money to go to California. He knew Chantrice had some money. When her first husband, Merrill, was killed in an accident at the mill, she collected quite a large insurance settlement, so Dennis decided to blackmail her instead of reporting the crime."

Elbert nodded. "That was his mistake. He did not know how ruthless she was."

Jenny picked up the story. "He called Chantrice the next day, told her what he'd seen. Told her he wanted five thousand dollars and he would go away. She told him to meet her by the woods in Wooster that night. She put some money in a bag and showed it to him. While he was looking in the bag, she hit him, killed him with the mallet. She put him in the car, stuffed the mallet under the seat, drove him up the old road and ran the car over the cliff. She thought when they found him, they would find the mallet with Emma's blood and Dennis's blood and it would lead them back to Jacob. But, like Emma, they never found Dennis."

"Chantrice didn't know that Jacob had buried Emma in the box," Bobby said. "She was sure the police would find Emma's body and arrest Jacob. When it didn't happen, and she had to give an answer if someone asked about Emma, she made up the story about Emma running away with Dennis. Even Sheryl believed it. Then when those boys found Emma, everything came apart."

Jenny nodded. "There are some crimes where the perpetrator never gets caught because the crime never comes to light. They are the smart ones. But most criminals make foolish mistakes because they react to situations instead of thinking them through. Once the boys uncovered the box, things fell into place that Chantrice had no control over. And then she started making mistakes. Her first one was keeping the bracelet when she heard about the dead girl and knew it was probably Emma. She should have taken it down to the river and thrown it in."

Rachel shook her head. "But where did Gary Walker come in, Uncle Bobby?"

"Chantrice knew Gary through some friends of Johnny Edwards. When they discovered the body, she knew right away it must be Emma, especially when the news about the quilt came out. She had Gary burn down the storage building where Doctor Garner kept his records to keep the police from identifying Emma that way. Then when Rachel and Daniel came, she had Gary try to steal the box at the station. She was worried that Mama would have kept a record of the quilt she made for Chantrice. But by doing that, she let us know that someone, probably the killer, was trying to interfere. Another mistake. Then she got Gary to make the threatening phone call. He spoke German so Jenny would think it was someone from the Amish community trying to keep a lid on things, you know, to keep the Amish from being drawn into a scandal. But it didn't work."

Bobby smiled. "No, it did not. We did not buy it. That call just confirmed to us that the killer was still around, so Jenny and I turned our focus back to Apple Creek."

"Chantrice had seen my mama's box when she was young," Jenny said. "She knew how meticulous Mama was. And then it became common knowledge, and she knew we were interviewing people to find out who the girl in the box was. So, she sent Gary to steal it. She couldn't have known my mother had torn the page out of the book with her name on it."

"And if that little corner with Chantrice's last name hadn't stayed in the book," Elbert said, "we might not have known who Jerusha gave the final quilt to."

Jenny nodded. "Getting Gary involved in the first place was another mistake. If she had left well enough alone, Bobby and I would not have known that the killer was still around. Then after he did those jobs for her, Gary must have put two and two together, and like Dennis, he decided he could make a few bucks blackmailing Chantrice. A fatal error on his part."

Elbert spoke again. "She knew Gary was strung out on heroin, so she mixed up a little present for him and brought it that night when he was expecting a payoff. We found the rest of the heroin laced with strychnine in her attic."

Rachel took a sip of coffee and then set the cup down. "What I don't understand is how Chantrice stayed on top of all the details of the case. I mean like knowing I was coming, where we were staying, you know, all that."

Jenny shook her head. "Remember, Chantrice lived only ten minutes from the village, so she had her ear to the ground. The Amish community tries to be private, but just like every other community, there are gossips and news spreaders. Chantrice probably had many people she knew who were close to the Amish. When the news about me coming with Bobby got out, she knew about it because the sheriff had already let the Amish elders know Elbert was bringing in some help they could trust. Good politics, but bad for our case. Thanks to him, it didn't take long until the entire community was in on it."

Daniel looked over at Elbert. "What will happen to Chantrice, Elbert?"

Elbert shook his head. "That's hard to say. There is no statute of limitations on murder in Ohio, so they will try her for all three murders. Of course, the childhood abuse may figure in the case. She will have a psychiatric evaluation to see if she's even fit for trial. She's not a young woman so she will most likely spend the rest of her life in prison or a mental institution for the criminally insane. One good thing has happened to her, though."

"What's that?"

"The *bisschopf* came in today and told me that the Amish community has raised several thousand dollars to help with her case. They can't reinstate her to the community because of the murders, but they consider her one of their own and they will help her in every way they can."

"That's wonderful," Jenny said. "And what about Jacob?"

"Well, that's going to be a little dicey. Jacob did not technically commit a murder, but by burying the body and staying quiet all these years, he became an accessory to murder after the fact. And like murder, there is no statute of limitations for that crime. Like Chantrice, he will probably see some jail time. How much, given the circumstances—that he was set up to think he killed Emma—will be up to the judge. In Jacob's case, they might be a little more lenient."

Rachel leaned over and took her mother's arm. "Well, Mama, you solved your first case. How does it feel to be the first Amish amateur detective?"

Jenny smiled and shook her head. "I found it very interesting. But there were things that happened that I can't account for. Like Elbert inviting me to help when I was the only person in the world who would know who made that quilt. Finding the ring that the coroner almost overlooked. And the few boxes of Doctor Garner's files that had Emma's records still in his garage. The two boys who just stumbled on the box, and Chantrice wearing the bracelet just that one time. And then there was the time in Jacob's shop when I asked the Lord to help and he sent a single ray of sunlight to show me the missing fish charm. Those things were acts of providence, as though the Lord wanted the case solved so that Emma could be put to rest. Very interesting. Something to think about when I'm back in Pennsylvania."

Bobby grinned. "I have one last question."

"What's that?"

"Is the cherry pie as good here as it is at Fisher's?"

They all laughed. Elbert shook his head. "I guess we better find out."

∼

THE NEXT MORNING, as they were getting ready to go, Jenny took one last walk through the house.

So many memories! And now, even more.

Rachel came into the kitchen where Jenny was standing. "Ready, Mama? Everything's packed in the truck, and Henry's waiting to say goodbye."

Jenny ran her hand along the kitchen countertop that her papa had made for Jerusha. Sanded smooth and then worn by years of use, it was still beautiful. The fall sun came through the window and brightened the room, and for a moment, Jenny did not want to go. She sighed.

Rachel put her arm around her mama. "I know, I miss them too. They were so good to me. Cousin Jarod said we are welcome to come stay in the house any time. Who knows?" Rachel grinned. "Maybe you'll get another case in Apple creek."

Jenny laughed. "Well, I don't know about that." She looked around one last time and then took Rachel's hand. "Okay, I'm ready."

They walked outside to the porch. "Give me a minute," she said, and she walked down to the old porch swing. She sat for a moment and let the years slip away.

I solved a lot of problems in this old swing. Wonderful memories.

Jenny got up. Henry was standing there, and she reached up and gave him a hug. "Keep an eye on the house for me, Henry."

"I surely will, Jenny. I surely will."

Jenny looked down at the group gathered at the bottom of the stairs. "Okay, let's go."

Just then, a police car rolled into the driveway and Elbert climbed out. "Good! I caught you before you left. I wanted to thank you all for the incredible help you were to me in solving this case. And just to let you know how grateful Wayne County is, here are your consulting checks and a letter of commendation from the sheriff." He shook Bobby's hand, and then Jenny's. He looked down and cleared his throat.

"So, Jenny."

"Yes, Elbert?"

"Do you think if I run into any more cases like this one, I can give you and Bobby a ring?"

Jenny looked at Bobby and grinned. "If you're sure you want to deal with an old Amish woman and a retired sheriff, we might consider it. But let's take it one case at a time, Elbert. One case at a time."

∼

More Porch Swing Mysteries to come! Stay tuned.

Do you want to find out more about Jenny Hershberger and

how she came to Apple Creek? Read the Apple Creek Dreams series—Find it here on Amazon: The Apple Creek Dreams Series

Do you want to find out more about Rachel and the rest of the Hershberger women? Read the Paradise Chronicles Series—Find it here on Amazon: The Paradise Chronicles

ABOUT THE AUTHOR

Patrick E. Craig is an award-winning author with eighteen published novels. He has won five CIBA Book Awards, a Selah Award and a Word Guild Book Award. His work includes six Amish novels, three World War II historical novels with a short story sequel, two anthologies of Amish stories, a standalone novel and a memoir, and two YA paranormal books. He lives in Idaho with his wife Judy.

MORE BOOKS BY PATRICK E. CRAIG

A Quilt For Jenna

The Road Home

Jenny's Choice

The Amish Heiress

The Amish Princess

The Mennonite Queen

The Journals of Jenny Hershberger

The Mystery of Ghost Dancer Ranch

The Lost Coast

The Gettysburg Letter

The Amish Menorah and Other Stories

A Christmas Collection

Say Goodbye To The River

Far On The Ringing Plains

The Scepter And The Isle

Men Who Strove With Gods

Beyond The Red Hills

The Drive

∽

Contact Patrick at pec@patrickecraig.com

Website: https://www.patrickecraig.com

Patrick's Amazon Page : **https://tinyurl.com/y3nwsmgs**

THE APPLE CREEK DREAMS SERIES

Book 1—*A Quilt For Jenna*

Jerusha Springer has spent months making the most beautiful quilt anyone in Apple Creek, Ohio has ever seen, and she knows it is going to take first prize at the Quilt Fair in Dalton. The prize money will be her ticket out of the Amish way of life—away from the memories of Jenna, the daughter she lost a year ago and Reuben, her tormented husband, who has been missing since Jenna's death.

On the way to the fair, Jerusha gets caught in the Storm of The Century. An accident leaves her trapped in her driver's car—and trapped by the memories of her marriage to Reuben and the loss of little Jenna. And then another littler girl enters the story and takes Jerusha's heart captive in a way she hadn't expected. Can this child also be the one to heal Reuben's pain as well?

A beautiful story of loss and redemption.

Book 2—*The Road Home*

Author Patrick Craig continues the story of Jenny Springer, the child rescued in A Quilt for Jenna, with a story of reconciliation and healing.

Jenny Springer is the local historian for the Amish community in Apple Creek, Ohio. When Jenny was a child, Jerusha Hershberger Springer rescued her from a terrible snowstorm, and when no trace of Jenny's parents could be found, the Springer family adopted her. Since then, the burning desire in Jenny's heart is to find out who she really is.

Then Jenny meets Jonathan Hershberger, a drifter from San Francisco who lands in Apple Creek fleeing a drug deal gone wrong. Intrigued by an *Englischer* with an Amish name, Jenny offers to help him discover his Amish roots. When together they dig into Jonathan's past, Jenny gets serious in her own search for her long-lost parents. And as they travel The Road Home together, Jenny finds the truly surprising answer to her deepest questions, while Jonathan discovers his need for a home, a family, and a relationship with God.

Book 3—*Jenny's Choice*

Jonathan and Jenny Hershberger are happily settled in Paradise, Pennsylvania on the farm Jenny inherited from her grandfather. But when Jonathan disappears in a terrible boating accident, Jenny and her young daughter, Rachel, return home to Apple Creek, Ohio to live with her adoptive parents, Reuben and Jerusha Springer.

As Jenny works through her grief and despair, she discovers she has a gift for writing. A handsome young publisher discovers her work and, after the publication of her first book, Jenny is on the verge of worldly success and possible romance.

Then a conflict arises with the elders of her church, and Jenny must ask herself if she's willing to go outside her faith to pursue her dreams. At the same time, the budding romance is at odds with Jenny's hope that Jonathan might someday be found alive. Jenny must choose and Jenny's Choice leads her to the surprising and heart-warming conclusion of the Apple Creek Dreams series.

THE PARADISE CHRONICLES SERIES

Book 1—*The Amish Heiress*

Rachel Hershberger's life in Paradise, Pennsylvania is far from happy. Her papa struggles with a terrible event from the past, and his emotional instability has created an irreparable breach between them. Rachel's one desire is to leave the Amish way of life and Paradise forever. Then her prayers are answered. Rachel discovers that the strange, key-shaped birthmark above her heart identifies her as the heiress to a vast fortune left by her *Englischer* grandfather, Robert St. Clair. If Rachel will marry a suitable descendent of the St. Clair family, she will inherit an enormous sum of money. But Rachel does not know that behind the scenes is her long-dead grandfather's sister-in-law, Augusta St. Clair, a vicious woman who will do anything to keep the fortune in her own hands. As the deceptions and intrigues of the St. Clair family bind her in their web, Rachel realizes that she has made a terrible mistake. But has her change of heart come too late?

Book 2—*The Amish Princess*

Opahtuhwe, the White Deer, is the beautiful daughter of Wingenund, the powerful chief of the Delaware tribe, and a true princess. Everything in her life changes when the renegade known as Scar brings three Amish prisoners to the Delaware camp. Jonathan and Joshua Hershberger are twin brothers that Scar has determined to adopt and teach the Indian way. The third prisoner is Jonas Hershberger, their father, who has been made a slave because he would not defend his family. White Deer is drawn to Jonathan but his hatred of the Indians makes him push her away. Joshua's gentle heart and steadfast refusal to abandon the Amish faith lead White Deer to a life-changing decision, and rejection by her people. In the end, White Deer must choose between the ways of her people and her new-found faith. And complicating it all is her love for the man who can only hate her.

Book 3—*The Mennonite Queen*

CHANTICLEER INTERNATIONAL BOOK AWARDS SEMI-FINALIST - THE CHAUCER HISTORICAL DIVISION: This is the third book in The Paradise Chronicles series. Isabella, Princess of Poland, is raised to a life of great wealth and leisure in the Polish Royal Court, destined to marry a king. But fate or divine providence intervenes when she meets Johan Hirschberg, a young Anabaptist who works in her father's stable. This chance meeting leads the young couple into a forbidden love. Together they flee Poland and embark on a dangerous journey that brings them, after great peril, to the small parish of a troubled priest named Menno Simons. Catholic Bishop, Franz von Waldek, paid by King Sigismund, Isabella's father to find the princess at all costs, pursues them across Europe. Isabella does not know it, but if von Waldek captures her, she will have to make a choice that will change the course of European history forever.

THE ISLANDS SERIES

Book 1—Far On The Ringing Plains

CHANTICLEER INTERNATIONAL BOOK AWARDS FIRST PLACE WINNER — HEMINGWAY 20TH CENTURY WARTIME FICTION.

Far On The Ringing Plains INSPIRED BY TRUE EVENTS In the spirit of The Thin Red Line, Hacksaw Ridge, Flags of our Fathers and Pearl Harbor. Realistic. Gritty. Gutsy. Without taking it too far, Craig and Pura take it far enough to bring war home to your heart, mind, and soul. The rough edge of combat is here. And the rough edge of language, human passion, and our flawed humanity. If you can handle the ruggedness and honesty of Saving Private Ryan, 1917 or Dunkirk, you can handle the power and authenticity of ISLANDS: Far on the Ringing Plains. For the beauty and the honor is here too. Just like the Bible, in all its roughness and realism and truthfulness about life, reaching out for God is ever-present in ISLANDS. So are hope and faith and self-sacrifice. Prayer. Christ. Courage. An indomitable spirit. And the best of human nature, triumphing over the worst. Bud Parmalee, Johnny Strange, Billy Martens—three men that had each other's backs and the backs of every Marine in their company and platoon. All three were raised never to fight. All three saw no other choice but to enlist and try to make a difference. All three would never be the same again. Never. And neither would their world. This is their story.

Book 2—The Scepter and The Isle

CHANTICLEER INTERNATIONAL BOOK AWARDS FINALIST — HEMINGWAY 20TH CENTURY WARTIME FICTION

It did not end with Guadalcanal. It did not end with one island. There were more islands... an island with snow-capped peaks, friendly people, blue seas, where Bud found love with his Tongan princess. Where Billy breathed the clean air of mountains where no danger lurked. Where Johnny found a way to drain the hate that drove him mad. They found life again after the death-filled frenzy of Guadalcanal But the God of war was not done with them. More islands sent their siren call from beyond distant horizons and they were cast upon dark shores. Islands with coconut palms, dense green jungle and death. Islands that took more life than they ever gave back. Islands where women killed like men, islands filled with the most brutal soldiers the Japanese Empire could offer. Tarawa. Saipan. Islands that had to be endured. Islands they had to survive. There was no other way to bring the war to an end. There was no other way to get home again.

Book 3—Men Who Stove With Gods

BOOK THREE OF THE AWARD-WINNING ISLAND SERIES. Since 1941 the Marines have fought the Japanese. They met them first on Guadalcanal, a maelstrom of death and fury. Tarawa, Saipan, Okinawa —their friends died beside them, their youth disappeared in a baptism of fire, but they kept on. Johnny, Bud, and Billy went ashore on bloodstained Okinawa hungry for the end of the war. But they knew when the battle ended, they would face their Armageddon on the sacred beaches of Japan.

PRAISE FOR PATRICK E. CRAIG'S BOOKS

"From the first page of *Jenny's Choice* I felt a tender compassion for Jenny, the young woman in this novel. Her story unfolds with a gentle hand and a lyrical tone that leads to an ending filled with hope. As with the other books in the Apple Creek Dreams series, you'll want to read this book in one sitting. Preferably with a cup of tea."

— **ROBIN JONES GUNN,** BESTSELLING AUTHOR OF THE GLENBROOKE SERIES AND THE CHRISTY MILLER SERIES

"Patrick Craig's Apple Creek Dreams series is both poetic and sincere. Strong characters who deal with the grief and joy of everyday life make these stories you'll remember long after you reach the last page....*Jenny's Choice* is a tender story of grief, restoration, and grace."

— **VANNETTA CHAPMAN,** AUTHOR OF THE PEBBLE CREEK SERIES

Patrick Craig writes with an enthusiasm and a passion that is a joy to read. He deals with romance, faith, love, loss, tragedy, and restoration with equal amounts of elegance, grace, clarity, and power. Everyone should pick up *A Quilt For Jenna*, his debut novel in Amish fiction, turn off the phone and computer and TV, and settle in for a good night's read. Craig's book is a blessing.

> — **MURRAY PURA,** AUTHOR OF *THE WINGS OF MORNING* AND *THE FACE OF HEAVEN*

A good storyteller takes a fine story and places it in a setting peppered with enough accurate details to satisfy a native son. Then he peoples it with characters so real we keep thinking we see them walking down the street. A great storyteller takes all that and binds it together with, say, a carefully constructed Rose of Sharon quilt and the wallop of a storm of the century that actually happened. *A Quilt For Jenna* proves Patrick Craig to be a great storyteller.

> — **KAY MARSHALL STROM,** AUTHOR OF THE *GRACE IN AFRICA* AND *BLESSINGS IN INDIA* TRILOGIES.

Made in the USA
Columbia, SC
28 May 2024